THE GHOST OF MEMORY

Wilson Harris was born in British Guyana in 1921, and came to live in London in 1959. His many novels include *Jonestown*, *The Guyana Quartet*, *The Carnival Trilogy* and *The Dark Jester*.

WILSON HARRIS

The Ghost of Memory

faber and faber

First published in 2006
by Faber and Faber Limited
Bloomsbury House, 74–77 Great Russell Street,
London WC1B 3DA

This edition first published in 2017

Typeset by RefineCatch Limited, Bungay, Suffolk
Printed by CPI Group (UK) Ltd, Croydon, CRO 4YY

A CIP record for this book
is available from the British Library

ISBN 978-0-571-34162-7

For MARGARET
ever and always

Author's Note

The Ghost of Memory is a novel about life and death or rather
– to put it somewhat differently – about the close, almost
indefinable cross-culturalities between moments of life and
death.

We know that life fades into death but in what degree does
life re-live itself as it dreams of dying?

We may dream, while still alive, of dying. But the dream is
soon forgotten as are the edges and corners of a re-lived life of
which we dream. It is buried in the unconscious.

Sometimes we may seek to unearth the buried dream. Such
an opening of the unconscious brings cultures from a collec-
tive (as C. G. Jung might well have put it) of which we had
little or no idea that we knew. There are surprises in store for
those of us who venture into a new consciousness of life
through the unconscious.

Anton Ehrenzweig in his book *The Hidden Order of Art*
states that 'the psychology of unconscious perception is still
unwritten'.

I have, in *The Ghost of Memory*, sought to bring 'unconscious perceptions' into play through a man who is shot as a
terrorist but who claims he is no terrorist and sees himself as
a sacrifice for the failure of a civilisation to recognise how it is
aligned to ancient rituals that feared the Sun might never rise
again and Darkness would engulf the world for ever.

This man is not to be taken literally. He is a dream-animal
who dies and lives in the dreams of Mankind at the edges of
consciousness and unconsciousness.

Similarly the Brain becomes the Sun of the body that rises within and without the body into a symbolic Light which governs all Mankind's actions.

The Mind is largely eclipsed and falls into Darkness that modern cultures seek to overcome through the unwitting sacrifice of those whose hearts and lives they still offer unconsciously to the Sun (or what passes for the Sun).

All this is traced in various ways through a narrative that has no absolutes.

The painting on the walls of a gallery, in a major City, carries the dream-animal or dream-man who falls into it and acquires phantom limbs that he conceals in a dialogue with one Christopher Columbus. He embodies the wisdom of the unconscious, that speaks to us with quantum limits that define the paradoxes of intuition.

That Columbus takes the name of *the* Columbus who arrived in the Caribbean in 1492. He is profoundly fascinated by the painting on the wall of a room, in the gallery, but he virtually hates it as it brings his unconscious into acute tension with his hard-and-fast convictions.

We are fleetingly aware that some of us seem protected, or cushioned in a haven of respite, while others are desolate or close to death in circumstances of grief or terror. To bring one and the other together requires an interplay, a close interplay, of the unconscious and the conscious wherein unconscious functions begin to attack, and bring down, egoistic surface sensibilities. This affords interior bridges between a moment of safety and another of desolation.

Equally we may be subtly aware that paintings and sculptures are animated by dreams springing from ourselves and from others. Paintings and sculptures would be wholly lifeless were it not for the mystery of the unconscious in the paradoxes of myth and uncertainty of sensation.

What is spirit? What is the New World? What is art? What is truth? What is evolution – how does it bear on the *leaps* that Man has made – without knowing for certain how they were made – and may still be drawn into making in the present or the future?

These are questions raised by the narrative, which it attempts to answer in implications of the immensity of the journey of life.

The artist may attack his . . . one-track thought; but a new order is already in the making.

Up to a point any truly creative work involves . . . the self-destructive attack of unconscious functions on rational surface sensibilities.

Anton Ehrenzweig, *The Hidden Order of Art*

Elena is earth seaweed
Ocean wave.

. . .

Standing on the rock and the coral of the
abysses.

Juan Sanchez Peláez, translated from
the Spanish by Guillermo Juan Parra

Art was a substitute through which one was involved, whether as a goddess or a god, to respond to multiple cries in the Silences of a numb humanity of wood or glass or flesh.

from *The Mask of the Beggar*

I had been shot. A bullet in my back. I fell. Where did I fall? I fell from a great height, it seemed, into a painting in a gallery in a great City.

I found myself returning across centuries and generations to the end of my age. I had been caught by the Artist in what seemed the womb of unexpected being in which one becomes sensitive to the end one has reached and to a new beginning. It was an end, it was a new beginning one was called upon to probe and discover.

It was wholly unexpected, hallucinatory yet real and confusing.

Was I a living Shadow or Reflection carrying a sudden message I would need to understand?

My Brain jumped alive in the canvas of space and became the Sun. Beneath was a great Darkness I had never seen before but it stimulated me fearfully.

I stood on an ancient River beside a great Forest. A stem or a broken leaf became a finger on my hand. It pointed to traces of infinity *within* itself, *within* other leaves on a tree. This *withinness* was a puzzle but it gave me a sensation nevertheless of how I had survived to fall from a great height into a work of Art painted in *still* lines differing in tone and colour but moving *within* themselves.

I set out along the River on a wave of land. Was it water or land on which I walked? The wave blurred my eyes. I felt awkward and uncertain of who I was, where I was. My bones which had fallen apart when I fell came into me from ditches sparkling with diamonds that turned into a shining fish (imagine a diamond-fish!) *drowning in air*. It had jumped to the water in the River but had been caught and held in a net. It fluttered like a living machine. Was it alive, had it drowned, was it dead? Such is a work of Art. *Caught like me.* Do machines drown in air with a bullet in their back or a hook in their mouth? I was *within* the many-sided fish, the fish or machine as it appeared in the painting was *within* me.

Art makes diamonds into the light of compassion on all things and creatures to reflect *dimly* (I would see it more brightly later) the perils of one (such as I) being shot, sliced, broken for the good of Mankind. *I had been shot because I was deemed to be a terrorist.*

Even with a diamond-sun, shining in the canvas of space, it was difficult to trace the heritage of fate in the humblest of creatures we take for granted on a stall or pedestal in the Market place.

In time – now that I moved within the womb of Art – I felt I would prove I was *not* a terrorist. I was Universal Man trapped like fish within the Market place of society.

The diamond-fish in the canvas of space was adorned with lines that could have come from the brain of a machine.

Beneath was the Darkness it would take me ages perhaps to see into with my night-eyes.

What I felt now – in the light of the diamond-sun – was the method I saw in use by men to articulate the height of the sky. Man discerned – in the drowning in air by a machine-creature longing to swim as designed by the gods – a way of finding an arch through a trapped body that could be lifted up to keep Darkness at bay.

Man would fashion a bowl from the caught wings (if I may so put it) of fish. Birds and fish became absolute food for technology and science to articulate the best way for flying in the sky. Birds were caught close to the River, as they attempted to swim into the air, and their stretched wings helped to measure the bowl of the sky in which it was safe for craft, for planes, to move without the danger of being lost in total Darkness. The Sun was kept aloft through such arches drawn from a heritage of fate. I would need to probe and understand this heritage much more closely as I moved along the River and the Forest.

I suddenly remembered the sculptor who sculpted me . . . He used his gun as a tool for the good of Mankind. His task or duty was dictated by the Sun which he defended in its material equivalents with fire, electricity, oil . . . Yet he had no vestige of imagination for the spirit of the serpent, or the fish, or the butterfly he crushed thoughtlessly in the palm of his hand. 'They have no voices,' he said. He could not hear them as they stirred dust in air and the singing rain in the River. The blow of the gun – though a betrayal of sight in not facing me whom he shot – was a stroke by a sculptor who sculpted without knowing that pedestals or stalls for small creatures match pyramids for sacrificed victims. Is the gunman an unconscious priest? Such is the visionary muscle of Art.

I was created Void, sliced, cut, but the Void turns and addresses the world in veil or mist. My lips are in the mist. I am maimed as I walk in spaces prepared by technologists as thresholds into height and depth. What is height? Do I embody falling multitudes? Am I within their fall? I say 'I' to register my ignorance of those who accompany me in an Art whose compassion is notable in the materials it uses to bring seeing light where blind light exists in cruelties engineered as normal everyday business.

I moved on the bank of the ancient River in the Forest. Leaves tipped into the fingers of others with me pointed to the stars emerging in the Sky. The Sun had been darkened in the density of trees that became a curious constellation in a Sky so close, it seemed, to Earth. Was it dark sun-rise or was it sun-set? I saw a leaf melting from a finger into a lip kissing a star. The star appeared to lean towards the lip of the Forest. The kiss was Void. The lighted star was millions of miles away. What then was I creating with my night-eyes in a Void of time, neither sun-rise nor sun-set?

3

The bright star came so close that it offered the strangest kinship to the Forest which congealed into a momentous head like an Olmec sculpture sliced from its rock-body of leaf-stone and upraised now with branched fingers mysteriously from the ground. A pre-Columbian miracle. Head, lip and hand in the ancient Forest.

Was such a kiss, between Earth and Heaven, the hallucination or the reality of complex Nature? The round Earth perpetually falls and rolls in the Sky as I fell instantly, it seemed, into the canvas of space.

My inner being, imbued with the traits of ancientness and modernity – within the grave of painting and sculpture or the womb of Art – was, all at once, driven by dreams and nightmares. Where did these come from? In the land? In the air? In the water? I felt myself astray on many paths on which a rapidity of questions came with each phantom footprint.

I found myself nevertheless with muscles, however nebulous, from the diverse paths I travelled. Vision needs the activity of thought. My night-eyes need an inner visionary muscularity to see through places and things.

Is this the truth of Art? Truth is stranger than Reason. This is human, profoundly human, but I felt that the all-too-human passion, encompassing death-in-life, was remote in a people largely divorced from the womb of Art.

I thought of the nets and arches in the bowl of the Sky fashioned by men. Each leap – drawn from the stretched wings of creatures – constituted an arch of safety. In the womb of Art I saw it differently. Each leap was a revelation of the gods in a conflict of ages between Darkness and Light. Darkness may possess a mystery that we need to comprehend.

An aircraft speeds, shapely as a bird, or a fish, in waves of cloud, in seas and mountains, also shaped like Cloud. I perceive, in a flash, the hidden god in the sparkle of metal wings and scales. The Sky becomes an umbrella raised above the Earth. Through well-nigh invisible holes in the umbrella – through which the eyes of the gods may be seen – there spew

4

forth tears, the tears one weeps for disintegration. Is this rain of pollution, raised above the Earth, an acknowledgement by a blind humanity of a Darkness above the Sun which matches the Darkness beneath? I see – with the eyes of the gods – the leaf and the lip in the ancient Forest – so close to the heavens – my fingers reach up and touch them.

What is the essence of action, what inner resources, outer resources, make action possible? What is man-made action, is it born through involuntary limbs in the web of life?

What is Nature's action, how definable is it?

When I fell I felt I fell from a great height I did not understand on land and air and water. I was on land. How could I fall from a great height? And yet the Void in space and time in the Artist's painting into which I fell, or was falling still, gave me a clue. One moves . . . One sits in a Void . . .

It seemed I had been pushed invisibly, or struck invisibly through the sculptor who had sculpted me, by a Titan or Master of Violence. Had the sudden blow given me hallucinations – reserved for those who are aware that they are dying – of falling from a pyramid or a high, ancient temple? Had it released the unconscious into a memory of past ages when pyramids were regarded as of immanent height?

This was disturbing, erratic, even stifling, as I fell, or was falling still, or seated still, in the huge canvas of space. It ran around the gallery on every wall. It was old, it was new. Had I truly fallen? Was I falling still? These questions revolved around me as in a dream of living and dying together in suspended sleep and waking.

Violence belonged to an inner commotion and to the bowl of the Sky painted with the tears of the gods. The Titan was blind to such tears, however seeing his eyes were. It was a trick of Nature, a liquid self-deception like water in a mirror with subtle waves that look unmoving and the same, left and right.

He arose into a Cloud, a Cloud that seemed so close to the ground it seemed to my eyes like a hill of paint or a giant

5

Master scrawled unevenly across the Sky. A god with airy features, foreign to dust and to Cloud, but taking delight in uneven iconography, may have hidden himself in him to give apparently firm texture to hills and mountains and seas congealed from nervous, slender atmospheres in a butterfly's pinned wing. Art reveals rigid superiorities through insects that are immortal paint.

Violence has many *tainted* shoes and garments, in which I dress, that fall from the bowl of the Sky. Am I a beggar? Am I a philosopher? Am I a revolutionary? All clothing is a mask through which my phantom body slips with inner muscles gained from diverse paths. The mirroring eyes of the Titan turn left and right with reversible changes that are so subtle, so painterly and silent, that few see the garment one wears as the strategy of paint to offset the glaring purity and simplicity of Titanic Reason which would burn for ever all reversibilities in its track.

Plato, the ancient Greek philosopher, sensed a grain of truth – in the chaos of original ideas in his time – by wearing mirroring eyes painted on him by the Artist. Light became shadow, shadow light, purity impurity, in the cave of his vision. It was an enigmatic approach to the Void of space. Within this Void, that he sought to measure in earthly terms, he perceived the fall of great Atlantis into an ocean of Dream.

The paint of the ocean stood left and right, up and down, like the cascading spectacles he wore. Did Atlantis descend into a Forest or a Swamp? Cries rose up some nights amidst the branched waves of Dream. The music of the abyss!

The Artist, employing characteristics of Nature, which deceive to enlighten, paints Plato afresh in the canvas of space as a radical philosopher and a conservative poet and scientist. Many emerge from this stem in the painting. I see them, in their new colours, watching the heavens within a cave of Earth *across the centuries*. Are they dead or alive, barely living perhaps, dying? They are drawn with a glory that men latch on themselves even if it is passing.

A philosopher sees the catastrophe of Atlantis as legend. So Cities are prized still for their gross materiality and modernity which Art wears to enlighten us to the abyss. It wears the prize that collapses in legend and in reality which we cannot distinguish one from the other. Nature continues to enlighten us still with eyes we never seemed to possess before in new and ever newer scrutiny of the living Self beyond glory's caves or graves or tombs.

A poet, or ape of Plato, sets a limit at the Moon. What is beneath the Moon is perverse, what is above is pure. This obsession, across the centuries, with dividing lines brings a sphere of blindness into every calculation. There are elements above the Moon that resemble birds caught in the Artist's brush. Legendary birds enlightening us to beating wings of time on earth and in heaven fallen and grown numb in the strategies of universal Art, *still* lines yet *moving*, impossible yet possible reality.

Such is Art beyond Platonic horizons.

Numbness takes us far into, *or within*, space and time. The timeless origins of space are sprinkled afresh, despite numbness, into unexpected, unknown universes. Not the massive dust and the Cloud in which the Titan broods but a vibrant reversibility of the numb in echoing strands of otherness.

Am I a part of that scattering of minute seeds which reaches through and beyond what is known as fixed regions? Is the massive Cloud of the Titan – with its hills and mountains and seas – a fixed region though it exists in a butterfly's wing? The gods are subtle in their revelations of legendary opposites that help us to see *through* ourselves.

It came on me suddenly that within the womb of Art, within the mother of Art, every universe is built on a fluid self, tempered with particles of Mind that may restore lost limbs. Art is a medium of insoluble life.

Does consciousness fall perpetually towards the unconscious of Dream encompassing many ages? Does one fall perpetually towards the grave in fire, in water, in earth, all painted as passages to life? Fire, earth, water are known to Nature but we exclude them from ourselves as un-natural, as acts of God, whereas they may be in unconscious relationship to ourselves in mute signals beneath colour and shouting line. Is there an inner mobile form within frames or parochial destinies? Consciousness (which we appear to know), the unconscious or hidden (which we appear not to know) need to be perceived or written in various ways.

I felt myself falling perpetually when I was shot and maimed. This was a human dilemma of life-in-death, death-in-life in obscure horizons. I was moved to look even more closely into the canvas in which I seemed to walk and to sit. I was pushed, it seemed, to read the Titan's eyes again. The Titan was the father of the gods. His sons left him to embroider the Fear that such fathers portray. It was an act they bestowed to Art to enlighten generations by slow and painful degrees that are a measure of human limitations. His eyes were drawn in curious and secretive depth which I had not noticed before and I was shaken with astonishment, shaken by the unconscious in the conscious.

Had this secrecy of Nature always been there in the spaces into which I fell? The canvas was undergoing changes that were new. Or my eyes were touched by visionary, all-too-human alterations. All-too-human in that one remembers walking in a street, before one was shot, a hundred times and more, and thinking one sees everything that is to be seen. Until a moment comes when one sees something that one cannot believe has always been there. Has it always been there? Has it not always been there? The street is a miniature canvas in which one exercises *phantom* eyes that one feels we may have possessed in some forgotten genesis with the promise of a wholeness we do not now understand.

This lost understanding makes us cynical of anything that crosses our material horizons and we extinguish every flash that comes fleetingly to us – indeed fleetingly from *within* ourselves – from without/within our rifled premises of behaviour and conviction. In that sense we all share the rifle that wounds the body of the Mind. 'I' am 'we', 'one' is 'another' in a range of fluid and original possibilities, a unique community in which the magic of wholeness intrudes . . .

I touched the Titan's eyes to see whether fresh paint would appear on my fingertips. Phantom fingertips! The wound I had received had made me more sensitive than ever not only to my limbs, back, body but to millions who had perished instantly in volcanoes and earthquakes. I was a phantom assembly in the canvas of space sharing a knowledge of the devastations of Nature that bring us back to the fleeting origins of creation within/without ourselves.

The grief I felt was real, as real as life, the life of the Mind. Mind has ancient sorrow it does not understand, fabrics of sorrow that reach through rational experience, Mind has sadness, joy, tragedy, comedy, interlaced in indescribable ways, Mind has vestiges of everything as it longs to return to the end and the beginning of things. It longs to return to a ground of truth, in which justice lives beyond all reasoning, absolute barriers. Mind longs to return, in sacred ships, to the promise of wholeness on a distant shore which is still there when an age collapses. There is a ladder between the shore of earth and the shore of heaven in the Artist's painting. We are astonished to see there a curious solidity to grief in painted lines, a nervous solidity to joy, to sadness, a strange arm shaped like the branch of a tree, a strange foot cut adrift in the storm of a battle climbing and falling from a ladder, a heart beating still with joy and sorrow that mount and achieve a fragile body for arm, foot and heart. Is the ladder a means of assembling the *height* of a solidity of feelings in Art? I touched the Titan's eyes once more as I climbed the ladder in search of *height*.

The paint lay on my fingertips. Who, I wondered, would see this articulation of grief, sorrow, sadness subtly and secretly given in paint as part of an immanent body, an unconscious/conscious body?

9

So much is missed by spectators who do not sense that Art lives afresh in them, dreams afresh in them, thinks afresh in them. They would see me as wholly fragmented or as a piece of entertainment. They would *not* see me as all-too-human.

I felt myself linked nevertheless to such blind/deaf spectators – as though blindness and deafness had solidity in Art – and they (the spectators) stood in the painting on the huge wall in the gallery on which the canvas was laid. I called on them silently to feel what was happening to me – as it was happening to them whether they knew it or not – I called on them to touch my fingers on the Titan's eyes.

Numbness would partially vanish in them if they responded to my cry. They too would find inner bodies tingling. They too would be astonished by the Mind's reach.

The Titan's left eye had gone underneath, the right stood now beneath the massive, violent portrait of a head. Violence looked deep into itself and changed subtly. All this was done so secretly, so hiddenly, few perhaps would feel touch had been allied to visionary warnings in phantom bodies.

Would this lead them into the subtleties of painted, unfinished being? Would the bullet in my back enter theirs invisibly but potently?

A change, I felt, was occurring in the Titan. Difficult to describe despite what I have already hinted at in telling of violence probing violence and seeing itself in virtually unconscious reverse.

Was the Titan a ruler of Mankind? Not *the* truest guide whom we perceive, let us say, in flashes in Art's legendary hand, Nature's hand on the ladder between the shore of earth and the shore of heaven. Yet the Titan is to be reckoned with. He has fashioned Fear across many centuries. His secret eyes are slowly affecting the hidden re-visionary personality of an age. There is a congruence – though we do not see it – between the Titan's eyes and our eyes . . .

The Art of Limbo deals with hidden visions. The Art of Limbo deals with the unconscious. It enters the Artist's painting. I see its entry in lines that dazzle . . . Yet they look, in another spirit, cold, hollow and inhospitable, as though the Artist's brush is uncertain of climate and mood in reversing the power of violence and greed and narrow interests. Yet in truth (when one studies the stroked lines closely, as they rain from the palette of Art, however eccentric they are) they bring new possibilities, within the Titan's eyes, they bring revolutionary spaces unforeseen by conventional logic.

Limbo fuses contradictory spaces shining darkly and strangely under the Titan's gigantic cover. Ghosts of memory still emerge, gnostic ghosts perhaps. No more than ghosts. I know for I am a ghost of memory myself. The Titan remains in perfect command on his cover or mask, in his dress that seems untainted. His eyes of the unconscious, the reverses in violence, are hidden and concealed. He has his armies, he constrains many, who are unwilling to join his forces.

As I climb the ladder I find myself on a pinnacle that has two sides, one is hope, the other is despair. I had sensed revolutionary spaces in the Art of Limbo. But revolutions in the past have led to resurgences of tyranny. Revolutions have been obliterated. There has been an American revolution, a French revolution, a Russian revolution, a Chinese revolution. Nothing remains but narrow conservatism, complacency, democracy under the banner of crude capitalism.

The Art of Limbo promises to dig deep, where no one has dug before, for reverses of violence within the Titan's eyes beneath his gigantic cover or mask, beneath his *untainted* dress, to dig deep into Fear, Fear of the grave, and to stir a seed within the womb of Art, the mother of Art beyond every formidable portrait of command we erect in space.

I found it still virtually impossible to know what is the great height from which I fell into the Artist's canvas (as though I am painted there by the hand of Nature). Perhaps I am somewhat closer to a psychical understanding of the mystery of height on the ladder and elsewhere in my close involvement with the Artist's creativity.

Dying into creativity may prove a threshold into an existence that passes away and comes into other levels of consciousness. One dies many times perhaps as one lives . . .

Am I a legendary, ghostly sacrifice on a pinnacle of hope? Is that pinnacle a pyramid of the Sun – a monument to the Sun – in Mexico or Peru? Such ancient, ghostly rituals were supervised by a priest who slid a knife into the victim's chest and extracted a heart, beating still, which was given to the Sun.

An invisible, ghostly knife runs across centuries into a soldier's bullet or bomb that devastates scores or thousands, into the Market place as well, in its stalls and pedestals, where the humblest creatures may be seen.

An exquisite knife was the tool the priest used on the pyramid of the Sun in Teotihuacan (the place where the gods are made). The gods or the sons of the Titan reveal an atrocity committed to keep Darkness at bay. Fear of Darkness, Fear that the Sun may never rise again when it sets inspires the priest who selects a naked heart beating in anguish. Yet such atrocities, such anguish, lift one into a privileged sacrifice that one bears for all Mankind. The gods deceive by upholding privilege, by upholding pinnacles, but in revealing the promise of sunrise-in-sunset they bring a Void into space and time. The Void had edged its way into the mystery of height but no one perceived it. A crucial edge, a crucial moment! It brought risks, grave risks perhaps, but an immense opportunity to conceive a dying into creativity. Fear was too strong, Fear of absolute Darkness, it was so strong the priest slipped the body he had sliced down the pinnacle of the Sun. Did I fall with that body and am I now trying to conceive what it is to be creative as I fall from the pinnacle into a painting?

Is there a Void in modern cultures? Global warming springs into a Void. Rising seas and changing climates are legend (as these now stand in people who dismiss them) and hidden realities pointing to disaster. The unconscious lives in the conscious whether we know it or not. Are we complacent? Do we fight to preserve an Economy that brings the promise of wealth for all, for the poor who long to be better off, for the rich who long for more riches? The hopes of the poor may be cancelled unconsciously perhaps by the rich who have no Mind for anything else but accruing riches.

The Artist presents such a Void with a decline in creativity, an irony that deceives and reveals, the promise of sunrise-in-sunset, the promise of ice as ice melts on the ladder and its Poles.

The Artist seeks the genesis of creation against a dying climate of mood, spirit and reality but the complex and far-reaching change he introduces is construed in purely economic terms.

The Art of Limbo enters creation by way of knives, tools, guns, technologies we have never considered as symbols of blood. *The knife slides into one's chest, the bullet into one's back*. The Art of Limbo paints rising seas with apparently frozen lines. Paint is a measure of stillness, of the still line, still knife, gun, tool. By such stillness Art perpetuates a continuity that no one understands between ancient and modern traditions of blood-consuming politics and religions.

13

Is the still line in the Artist's painting a deception concealing profoundest movement, profoundest heights, across the ages? Every small but far-reaching rise in swollen seas tells us, with Art, of dangers we underestimate in failing to respond to intimate truths presented in a grain or an inch.

The Artist's painting I see – as I look at myself from within it, as I breathe magically, it seems, and wonder at the air between the lines – comprises grains and inches.

The deceptions of the gods are as present today as yesterday – in ancient symbols which presented the appearance of a living Sun – as they are present in abstract symbols of a modern Economy in which the Sun relates to us through electricity and computers that interlace into the fire of a Brain.

The Sun out there I feel is native to humanity in the philosophy of ancient Mexico. It led to blood as an equation between Nature and Man. Nature was feared, Man was privileged to keep Darkness at bay in surrendering his heart's blood. Blood is both visible and invisible in the Artist's painting, visible as an ancient food of the Sun, in the veins of creatures, invisible as the waters of the Earth and in symbols of a modern Economy.

Blood is high wages, electricity, oil. Blood is terror, terrorism. Blood congeals into a bullet or a bomb fired into space like an arrow of pointed rain joining the waters of Earth in a meditation on a battle, or a murder, or an assassination, *or a flood*.

The waters link themselves into human desecrations in the Artist's canvas to keep us abreast unconsciously (if not consciously) of the ruin of ourselves in violence that impinges everywhere and is mirrored in turbulent, boisterous floods.

Nature cries out in a cry that is eloquent with many voices within bird and beast and forest. But how can the Artist truly paint such a cry except in a serpent's voice or within a flower that fades and blooms? The cry I utter is voiceless within spatial, mothering lines that cry with me in Art that *sees* many voices in *painted* sounds.

And then I hear another cry, the cry of *terrorism* that shakes me. Does it arise from within myself or from within voice and voicelessness?

There are obscure lines suggesting oppositions that are assumed to be lethal to an established Economy with grooves in the suffering Earth.

Fear of opposites is denied by the modern Economy but maintained as dangerous in the psyche. How fearful is the psyche? The psyche is silent, yet it utters a cry. It seeks to justify its Fear in uncertain and ambiguous lines that are in some disarray. Is it a Fear that pinnacles and towers may suddenly be demolished bringing a Darkness of psyche on the land? The psyche is *within* the body and it resembles the Darkness in ancient Teotihuacan. The Sun must be fed to ensure its rising again. The pinnacles and towers must be guarded in modern Economies with planes, with bullets, to keep everything in place. Except that each guard becomes an iron priest awaiting the approach of those it would sacrifice to protect the world of innermost, crying psyche. 'Its psyche is the psyche of the free,' the iron priest implies. I find myself shaken, on the edge of a Darkness I do not understand . . . There is no sharing of Fear with the enemy as the Earth shares its floods with human well-nigh indescribable passion in the caught wings of birds on the ladder of space. The trap is on both sides, *within* the two sides like a subtle abyss I must wrestle with to understand . . .

Can I wrestle with it and not open myself to terror and Fear? The Artist rises within me and offers chances I cannot evade . . . The enemy is driven by hate. I see this in the painting. He plots – as if he knows a part of me that is desolate – to destroy towers and pinnacles and bring them into the abyss of Atlantis. He relates unconsciously to Plato, to me, and to the iron priest. I see him vaguely emerging, as in a dream, and then descending into the victim with a bullet in his back.

Who is the victim? The figure in the painting changes again. Am I that victim? I ask myself – as I sense many faces in myself – where does the victim truly belong? Is he universal despite divisions of fearful freedom and of enmity? Does he die (as everyone dies again and again in a dreaming life) and fall into other levels of consciousness?

The Artist had painted the Titan as father of the gods. His sons had abandoned such a spectre of power and cruelty *evolving* now, it seemed, in him and in themselves into maternal wisdom that they thought might help them to respond to the limitations of humanity. Humanity tended to be cruel and to seek power by every means. The abstract eyes in the Titan's violent head were a revelation of possibilities in dimensions and visions.

Who is the Mother if the Titan is the Father? Is she a hidden archetype *within* Egypt, within Greece, within Mexico or Peru or Europe or Africa or India? She could have sprung from any of these *withinness* sources or from others. The Artist has painted her with such spatial lines that I find myself naming her the Mother of space. Space is amorphous and large but it is minute as a shell of breath at the bottom of the sea or up in remote legends on the ladder on which I now stand. This signifies I feel that the Mother gives access to the core of all peoples . . .

Her spatiality in the painting opens enormous questions of universality and protection unlike the narrow curvature of the Titan who is still served with blood. The Titan and the Mother are differing yet related aspects of equations between Nature and Man.

She is fed or served with bread that breaks apart and has the blood of labour within it. Bread is a design which brings crumbs of *evolving* wisdom into play. Each crumb is small, so small it is ignored or forgotten in assessing the origins of Art. The evolution of Art, it seems to me, is immense . . . Is *evolution* the best term?

In parallel with seemingly human markings, in paintings or on a sculpture, Nature has a line I am scarcely able to see from conception through a foetal region into the birth of Man. On

16

that line, in which one thing looks like another, the soul or young brain (the dawning Sun in the body) is placed in the foetal region two or three months after conception. But in a painting with crumbs of wisdom, in a state of perpetual evolution, those months are dark ages, strangely terrifying, in the womb of Art.

I am dumbfounded, I am on the lip of Fear, but I seem to hold Fear in a state of perilous arrest, as I ponder the lines that jump from Nature to Art and back again. The Mother seems to jump across the abyss that I see. She touches seeds within Nature, she touches breath in the brain of Art. Yet there is a chasm or abyss between appearance and reality, between brain and breath. How may I cope? I console myself with the following musical adumbrations on the ladder of space.

There is a subtle musical abyss between the Mind of Art and the Brain of Art.

A drop of water, shining dark and light, iridescent, sings on the leaves of a tree. It is an eye of immemorial Mind across ages. Limbo hushes into a whisper but drops its cold knives, guns, bombs into the Brain. Is the Brain young or old? Brain has skills that have placed cities around the globe in a concert of ruin engineered by orchestras of conflict and waste.

I am taught by maternal wisdom to weigh my phantom eyes in minute solidities of music on the ladder on which I now stand.

I am taught to weigh a grain as indispensable to a painted bullet. The grain exercises a matchless concert in paint with bullet. The two are the same – grain and painted bullet – and yet so utterly different grain becomes a drop of falling music and the breath of Art in a rain of mind. Mind is absolute . . .

I was suddenly filled with virtually paralysing Fear. The Fear I had partially anticipated – however apparently illogical – had materialised.

I had said to myself – *Mind is absolute* – and had deceived myself in the sublime reverie and beauty of poetry embodied in Everyman. Who am 'I'? Who are 'they'? Who are 'we'?

There was a commotion between the conscious and unconscious. I saw now suddenly, in the Artist's canvas, not only the commotion in lines, but I gained a sense, which distressed me, of the immense, inner turbulence cultures experienced (whether ancient or modern) in seeking to overcome a dread blanket they anticipated if the Sun should not rise again. The Darkness that rose up staggered me. Did it rise from my attunement of Mind with the breath of a line? I felt this to be true of a work of Art. Did this Darkness rise inevitably in a Self-of-Art that was unfinished in the way the Brain, on a fragmented line in Nature, becomes the Sun in a phantom body, phantom in a work of Art?

I had deemed Mind to be absolute and, in so doing, had endorsed unconsciously the rise of Darkness in which the origins of Mind were hidden. This filled me with terrible distress. How could I attune the Mind so beautifully and find I had given rise to a Darkness?

I had cancelled (without thinking across barriers where I may have seen the truth of Brain and Sun) all alternatives in Nature and Art. The abyss between Nature and Art carried such alternatives. I would need to look deeply into myself and others who were strange and alien, however beautiful they seemed.

Cancellation of alternatives was not my intention. One cancels without knowing the depths of what one cancels. I thought I was doing right. What is right, in one's sincerest intentions, may be fatefully wrong in one's limited understanding of the body transfigured by Nature and Art. *Yes, I had deemed Mind to be absolute* – Mind attuned to breath – in the way cultures had seen the fiery nerves of the Sun in involuntary kinship with the Brain (this seemed a hollow excuse for my blunder). Was it truly hollow? Was it more hollow than electric bulbs and computers that shone as the brain-sun of the modern age?

They (the ancient and the modern) were unconscious (I argued in myself) in that they extrapolated the *absolute lines and nerves of the Brain into the Sun, a Brain that was divorced from a true relationship with a conception of Mind.* But mind is not absolute. Here lay errors in poems that can deceive in their beauty.

None of this was seen or understood. Cultures had assumed the fire in the sky, the trees on the land, the waters and the rivers, were absolutes. They had not visualised the divorce of the Brain from Mind that rose up and tormented them.

Like me, they had made grievous blunders – without knowing it – and we would continue to do so in our short-sighted mirrors of reality.

Nature conceives afresh the perils of the Self, all within a body embracing fire and tree and water. Who could say what is phantom, what is real, as we embrace the world?

The body masquerades as the only real and absolute thing and sets up a victim, who seeks universality in new impossible/possible flesh, new limb, to be spun from the violations of the past into a future where it is no longer the truth to be sliced or shot or eternally maimed for Mankind. Yet such maiming is a way forward, in the circumstances of long-enduring fate, in which one faces contradictions and potentialities in approaching the mystery of the Self.

I must enter hallucinatory (and real) errors to find myself in a living, struggling humanity within the abyss of Art and Nature.

I had now come to a series of great and terrible rapids in the River I followed. I descended the ladder rising from the rapids and their waving vortex. The surfaces of the water shone with rock and pebble. The depths were a turbulent body of swirling tides. Nevertheless I was at peace in the magic of stillness. One looks into the rapids from beneath above. 'Beneath above' establishes cultural/psychical links with Nature. Thus one is not merely *describing* what one sees. One is within, beneath, above what one sees.

My eyes were blurred with painted vistas, vistas of water, lines of intimate, most slender rivers that became threads in the carpet on the floor of the gallery in which the painting and sculptures moved as if they followed a thread to encompass the great City. Spectators walked on these threads to meet me. Such is the height and the depth of a work of Art.

A car on a street in the City – the maze of the City – also moved by long, slow stages into the painting like a pebble, peering through the rapids, appearing more still than the board beneath the carpet on which it settled like a fragment, a broken vehicle, exhibited for a feature of style and fashion. There were spectators around it, around me, for I came up in the rapids and sat upon it. I sat with the visionary uncertainty of ages into which I had entered since I fell, ages that left marks upon me of a *stable* ruin or ruination. All things break and leave traces that never die in the rapids of history. These make for a stable ruin which one rarely sees in the boiling waters. These traces look tainted, for they tell of ages we have squandered when we say we are pure. We seek now through thread and pebble to find a new philosophy of regeneration without deceiving ourselves wholly about what we are. Trickster, philosopher, beggar, lover, wanderer, hero, thief, villain . . . Perhaps we share these traits and many more.

My night-eyes – associated with death – were in my day-eyes as in a Dream. I dreamt I had been far away in Darkness, a painted Darkness that acquires contours and edges of *light*. What *light* had I seen? A baffling *light* that looks like a distant star seen from a gnostic shore, a remote creation I had somehow entered even as I stood in this, in the rapids of history.

I rose now, once again, in the rapids and peered at the *light* I had brought with me. I saw it still. I had not seen it before in the painted edges of the canvas when I first fell. Was it a star? Ancient magi, approaching the stable in which Christ was born, had seen a star no scientist has been able to identify in a scrutiny of the body of the universe. Was it a star? Was it a *light* that sprang from a Darkness beneath a foetal region still implicit in the universe?

The foetus had matured into a Child, the Child of the universe. Sages down the centuries claimed the Child as *absolute*. Their Brain shone brightly as they did so. Yet they were baffled by the *light* the magi had seen. Scientists saw it as the light of a star which they sought across days and years to stable within calendrical approximations . . . It was a star existing where no star was to be found: sun-rise in sun-set . . .

It was a violent age that the magi had entered. Violence had multiplied across *titanic* centuries in the rapids of history. Perhaps if they had seen the *light* differently . . . I stopped. The voice of a spectator in the gallery addressed me – 'Nonsense,' it cried. 'Mythical nonsense. Do you see what the canvas is saying?' The shape of the spectator turned and addressed other shapes in the gallery.

'I shall speak to you later,' I replied, 'when I leap out of this painting in the tainted, ruinous dress of a philosopher and a beggar. I shall have to bring the pieces together. What is myth? Myth may be close to the strangeness of truth.' I had spoken rashly. The spectator was astonished to hear a voice he could not identify and he awaited my presence.

Where was I? I was everywhere in myth, in the rapids of history, but I scanned the ground closely, the threads in the maze that ran everywhere and concluded I was now in the Amazon or the Orinoco, a far way from the violence Herod perpetrated in his attempt to kill the Child of the universe. That Child had many sliced bodies in other children, sliced arms we have forgotten save as statistics of history. I look *through* the statistics of history at the violent ruins from which I sought my dress to respond to the spectator who had spoken in the gallery a moment ago.

There were Cities beneath the Amazon and the Orinoco basins. Abandoned and long forgotten. People had lived there but – for one reason or another – had fled and left the places to fall into ruins from which pieces emerged, so apparently insignificant, they had not been seen and had become passive.

Such is the mystery of cloth and canvas that are deemed to be nothing more than plaques for entertainment. They suffer neglect though a painting appears upon them with a Dream of life and death. No one knows how to approach life in its universality or how to approach death as a passage through the grave in the womb of Art. This is a question for legend *and* reality and we are a far way from apprehending what such duality means. An all-too-human predicament. A street in the City which we see and do not see, as a miniature canvas with legendary associations, is a thread in a maze of ends and beginnings that bear on uncertain reality.

Was the complex thread now arising – out of its passivity – lit by a Dream I had seen which enters a stable, universal ruin, drawn from different places in ruins, in which nothing dies entirely as it is a compass of traces of the past in the present and the future that seem absolutely new?

I wondered whether I could pluck something from under my feet to install on or in my dress.

The fragment of a car on which I sat brought me a pebble to wear at my chest. I sat on a car that peered through the rapids with my eyes that ran around it swiftly, a car that had been reduced to a pebble. I sat on it and I wore it simultaneously upon me as though my eyes moved around it and beyond it, it was part of me, it was marvellous and slight. I dreamt I lay with it in a painted grave in which I had buried all my secrets for generations and which now had a slight opening at its edges, no larger than a pebble, through which I was given room to fashion a door into space. Had I fashioned it or had it come from the living Earth, polluted as it was, and fashioned me? I shared an architecture in the Earth in which secret pebbled doors and walls were alive and opening voluntarily/involuntarily. Without such a sensation of secret openings coming to life, in odd pieces of ruined walls, one was doomed to endless imprisonment – to growing imprisonment – in structures and machines that were turning passive on grooved pathways. Was I a Trickster in Dream-land? Was I involved in far-reaching tricks of Nature and Art? Art depicts universal ruin in which all infirmities are priceless as they rise into another dimension of startling, living life. Left as an infirmity and nothing more they tell of the triumph of death. How do they arise? They arise in the womb of Art into which one falls from a great height, it seems. Who can say what that height is? Infirmities may have come through violence, the violence of spoilt Nature-in-Man but they may convert by a decision of true consciousness into what they appear not to be, into freedom rather than fate.

This subtle leap from infirmity brings into the Artist's painting curious figures of acute slenderness that are sliced, I thought, from material forms to participate in differences – different measures to eternity – with an infinite point that abhors violence. With the glance of an eye that seemed to move around these figures, and to give us an odd sensation of invisible roundness, I found my blurred vision clearing for a moment or two and passing through the rapids of history.

I was drawn now into the womb of Art by a vision of constellations. They had been placed there almost surreptitiously. They were surrounded by me – even as they surrounded me – in proportions that rose out of the ground, it seemed, as much as from remote heights far above the bowl of the Sky. Scattered stars came together in unexpected designs that were related to lights I could not identify. A mysterious relationship was established to cultures severed or battered into a ruin that was universal in its darkness, in its lightness, both shining with the aroma of paint. One's nose became an eye in paint.

Was such a relationship between Darkness and Light, between Sight and Smell, a premonition of the living *origin* of constellations? Did this disclose something of the Artist's creativity? Who could say where lay the origins of Art joined to the constellations?

I felt a dual meaning emerging in the edges of the canvas not only between Darkness and Light that I sensed as important or between original Art and the distant constellations but *within* visibility and invisibility in the mystery of space. What was I to make of a painted bull, a dog, a horse, painted Orion, painted Jason, and many others? Did these images come across vast distances to be copied by the Artist? Or did they come as skeletons without names in timeless spheres above and beneath me? Who can say whether those skeletons were Tricksters of light, Tricksters of the senses, that inveigled themselves into Art to baffle us about heights and depths? The stars that hold them in place may no longer exist across vast reaches in which it takes invisible light-years to reach us.

I had scarcely meditated on such distances that present themselves in Art through a Trickster or a reduction in material form, resembling but differing from absolute violence, when I was bowled over in the rapids and gained a bank of the River with the edges of my fingers (that still carried paint from the Titan's eyes). The River bank on which I climbed was unfamiliar to me. My fingers lost a grain of paint as I climbed on a high mound on this area of the land. Suddenly there emerged from behind the mound a group of naked people. They were painted in the colours of Nature, so much so they could have been the flakes from trees. Each flake came from the ancient Forest which had been demolished in places. In this spirit they brought traces of the past on their naked bodies. They held in their flaked hands what may have been the thinnest, most slender embodiment of the mother of their tribe. They held it with acute tenderness as if they were groping in the past and the present. Groping figures uncertain of themselves. Perhaps the motherhood they sought, or were seeking, had been lying on the ground and I had not seen it. I was stricken when they held it out to me, stricken by their generosity. I glanced at it and around it as though it extended invisibly into far spaces from which they had come in South or Central America.

The mother-figure was the epitome of slenderness with the frailest, leaf-like breasts. She was paint and she was sculpture at the edges of the canvas as though one slim form climbed through the other, a painted form through a sculpted form. Her throat was thin and elongated, her head small as a shapely nut and elegant in poise and reflection. I gasped with astonishment – Giacometti's *Standing Woman*! This reflection flashed on me in the light that shone on a masterpiece of sculpted line. Was it paint? Was it sculpture? Was it both? Whatever it was it did not hinder my glance from passing around it into spaces on the bank of the River through which the flaked tribe had come from broken and demolished Forests growing again perhaps, it seemed.

'Giacometti's *Standing Woman*,' I cried with paint in my voice. 'Thin, elongated body. Astonishing. Beautiful.'

There was a furious roar from a spectator. He was the only one in the room. The others had gone into different rooms in the enormous gallery.

'Myth and nonsense,' he shouted. 'Who would believe a primitive relic in the hands of ancient Arawaks – who look like felled, walking trees – is in any way akin to the important work of a twentieth-century sculptor? Do you really believe this – that Giacometti was influenced . . .?'

I stood at the edges of the canvas in the constellation of the Trickster. I felt remote and far away and yet spaces invited me to step into the gallery in my pebbled dress that had fallen from my chest along my body. I found myself standing beside the spectator who had shouted with such disdain and contempt.

'I never said', I cried, 'that he was influenced . . . But I felt that there was a resemblance of line. That is all. A curious resemblance that tells us of distances we have travelled in one shape or another to reach where we are. Those distances are there in a twentieth-century sculptor who is sensitive to material form as never absolute . . . By the way, you say that the tribe coming from behind the mound on the bank of the River are ancient Arawaks. How do you know?'

The spectator swung around and regarded me closely. At first he was puzzled by my appearance. How old was I? He could not say – forty, fifty, sixty. My face looked dappled. The pebbled dress concealed my phantom limbs completely and gave me the appearance of solidity. He could not say what ethnic stock I might have come from. I wondered in myself – could I have been created by the Artist as he gazed up above the bowl of the Sky? I looked at the painting and saw the pebbled Trickster. He should have disappeared when I stepped out of the canvas. But there he was. Was I real or unreal? An all-too-human dilemma. Do people know how real or unreal they are? At last the spectator regarded me as an ape of the Trickster in the canvas. I had put on a pebbled dress and had dappled my face.

'Who said I spoke to *you*?' he demanded. 'Where have you come from?' He did not wait for me to reply. He assumed I had come from a neighbouring room. 'I was speaking not to *you* but to the painting, to the Artist . . .'

'You said Arawaks,' I interrupted. 'How do you know?'

The spectator hesitated for a long while then he continued: 'I am studying this canvas closely. I come four or five times every week. This has been going on for months.'

'You are deeply fascinated,' I said calmly.

'Perhaps I am . . . I am a great admirer of Christopher Columbus. That is how I know that they are Arawaks.'

'You speak as though you *are* Columbus. He appears in the canvas later on.'

He hesitated again for a long while, then he spoke diffidently but with increasing self-confidence – 'I have changed my name. I am now known *as Columbus*. No relation to the great man. Just a change of name. It means a lot to me. Yes, it means a lot.'

He rushed on – 'Yes, they are naked Arawaks. Who would now credit it that they are one of the most remarkable cultures in the New World after the Mayas and the Incas? I do not believe this. Columbus met them in the Atlantic – they had not yet vanished in the Caribbean – and he wrote of them – "that they all go quite naked as their mother bore them". I feel *I* met them.'

'You met them, poor devils, and you slaughtered them,' I said softly, under my breath. 'The values of the Titan!' What do you really care, I thought to myself, for cultures that differ profoundly from yours? You may arrive on a new land and kiss the soil, a kiss that reflects on your own values and makes no allowance for theirs. The Titan's hidden eyes – that I have seen worn by Plato in the painting from which I have come – have the unconscious source of fascination that brings you to the gallery month after month, day after day. A fascination that grips you, despite yourself, despite your rebellion against the work of Art you come to study and to see. You have changed your name. You are known now as Christopher Columbus. You are staring at the mother-figure that the tribe has brought with them and which I hold with my other hands, as in a Dream, in the painting.

'Could *this* be their mother? I see it in new ways every day I come. But it's totally absurd.'

'Why is it absurd?' I questioned him. Did he see that the people had generously passed to me the mother-figure they bore so tenderly in their hands? Perhaps they thought it fitting for a ghost of memory to have such slender beginnings in a maternal wisdom that could become dominant in the extreme and needed to be thinned and sliced by the genius of Art. Could not a Child become the mother and father of the past unconsciously perhaps?

Did he see that I was a painter's, a dreamer's, vision of a twentieth/twenty-first-century man, with a bullet in his back, who had travelled to the end of his age in search of new beginnings? Did he see that I embodied, in visionary attire, thousands, millions, who had been shot, bombed, broken in the marketplace of history as enemies or terrorists of established states which terrorised in turn those they pursued? Perhaps he had glimpsed some of this and it made him resentful and inwardly fearful.

'Why is it so absurd?' I questioned him again. 'You are fascinated though you deny the Art that you see. I would say

27

that the slender mother-figure raises problems deep within ourselves, deep within the womb of Art, the slender mother-figure carries the pregnancy of space outside of herself, around herself . . .'

'Pregnant space! That's an odd one. What do you mean?'

'Children grow into adults,' I replied. 'They must change in some degree. Do they recognise what that change may mean? By and large they may not. They remain stuck in a fixed father and a fixed mother, they remain therefore in a state of permanent adolescence and immaturity. Whereas life has no such stopping point. We grow inwardly with new experiences. Father changes, mother changes. They change with a deeper experience of pregnant space, the line that runs into the world from a seed of conception to the birth of Animal and of Man which is never finished as an awareness of the limitations and extensions of ourselves. We are born and re-born within and beyond ourselves. We may care for our parents when they are ill. We may exercise great care. But the change that has happened in us means a new orientation in which we become virtually parentless. We need a wider and deeper relationship in which to employ ourselves. I am putting it awkwardly. What I am getting at is the genius of Art through and beyond all fixtures with which we would stop universal life in its tracks and claim we have an absolute solution to the ills of humankind. There is no such stopping point in a universe as strange as ours and unless we realise this all cultures will remain in a state of fear. They cannot face the deepest problems that have arisen and are arising . . .'

Columbus eyed me with incredulity. He could not believe what I was saying. Perhaps he saw me as a madman. Madness is the opposite side of profound creativity. As materialism is the opposite side of secret villainy. In a tight-fisted age where everything has been worked out with apparent efficiency – asylums for the mad, prisons for the villain – where fixtures and absolutes do not confess to their madness, creativity is banished and materialism triumphs as the sane procedure in punishing those who are so inept, so cruel, so violent, they have to be put away to protect us from the rage of inner Darkness that we fear. Columbus eyed me with incredulity, yes, but I thought I saw a gleam of faint understanding in the eye that was staring at me. The eye seemed to pop out of his head and look at me.

'You may say what you like,' he said, almost as if he were an automaton, eyeless for a brief moment, and could say nothing else, 'but I still find it absurd that the Arawaks should look on such a thin and wasted woman as their mother . . .' Modern and ancient sculpture, I thought, he has forgotten the link between the two. Creativity is not entirely banished . . . His voice broke into my meditation, his eye had returned into his head – 'They should conceal it from view as a sickness of being. They should put it in a mad-house. My mother and my father are a Church. They are eternally the same spirit. They never change. I worship them. *This*' – he was pointing at the canvas – 'is not a Church. It is less than a skeleton . . .'

I followed his pointing finger which was aimed at the skeletal mother-figure and pondered his remark, 'less than a skeleton'. Did he know that Art composed material bodies – that have become legendary – on the skeleton-constellations in distant skies? What was their origin in Nature? Was Art mad or creative? It was humbling to approach such skeletons again in modern and ancient sculpture. The paint was alive to give a sense of sculpture. But it was a beginning.

Columbus watched me quizzically. He said, 'It's funny but I have not seen you here before and yet you have made a close study of the canvas.'

'I come in the evenings,' I said. 'The gallery is very quiet then. I can think. I can dream.'

'Ah! Yes. That explains it. I leave before evening. You are an excellent . . .' he paused for a moment . . . 'yes, a truly excellent *ape* of artistic detail. I am not being rude, believe me. But I note how exactly you have copied details from the canvas. Even your finger-tips! I see it there on the canvas and I see it here on you. Your dress as well! Your face as well. Dappled with lines, as if with paint.' He was smiling now, a quick smile, as though he were suddenly thinking of something other than my appearance – 'Would you like to know who happen to be my spiritual parents? Through them I am here. Perhaps I am myself an ape, Columbus's ape.' He was laughing at himself now, laughing at history, but with a twist to his lips that set me on my guard.

'Who are they?' I asked. 'Who are your spiritual parents?'

'King Ferdinand and Queen Isabella.'

I was startled. He was laughing still. He had, it seemed, a strange sense of humour. This should give him a sense of his frailties, the frailties of an obsession, the frailties of history. Could those frailties leap into unexpected life? I saw again the twist at the edge of his lips. Was his humour tinged with arrogance and pride? Did he know that Ferdinand and Isabella were religious fanatics who ousted the Moors from Spain where they had ruled for seven hundred years with tolerance? Christians, Muslims, Jews mingled easily and worshipped as they pleased. All this came to an end with Ferdinand and Isabella.

I saw now that his humour had a slightly upsetting flavour. The Church never changes, he had said. It remains constant, despite political or historical uprisings. Was he poking fun at history, at political uprisings? Was he laughing at himself? Ferdinand and Isabella were military as well as religious leaders and had profited from such uprisings.

'Tell me,' he was saying, 'what do you make of the man who falls into the painting? He was shot, a bullet in his back, was he not? Has he been painted there before he fell? Does he see himself there as he falls? I see you are masquerading as that man. You have two lives then, one in the painting and one outside. As I have two lives, one in Christopher Columbus and one outside. History is a canvas as well, depending on the biases of the state that reports events.'

Yes, I thought, he does realise who I am but as a masquerader who comes in the evenings to study the canvas and to make myself into a copy of what I see.

'It's a Dream,' I cried, 'we dream of dying while still alive.'

'Do you come to this canvas because of your dreams? Am I dreaming?'

'We are enacting the dreams of humanity. You dream of Ferdinand and Isabella and you act as though they are spiritually alive even though you laugh at yourself. You dream of Christopher Columbus and you act to change the world through him, through his name that you have taken upon yourself. Many people do this but they do not confess to the names that drive them.'

'Are we both dreaming? It's incredible. I do not believe it. It's easy to surrender ourselves to a Dream. Why do I come to the canvas? I come because I see new things I never saw before. I need to sort out my senses even though I know what I am doing is right. *The Artist is a Trickster. Is the man whom he paints, who has been shot, also intended to be a Trickster?*'

'Dreams are never easy. They are hard to understand. We are all riddled with paradox. We deceive ourselves and reveal ourselves. There are inexplicable events in history. Some see the Virgin in the Christian panoply and doctrine of holiness. Hallucinatory or real? They see her while others stand around and do not see her. Some believe Christ rose from the dead. Few recognised him. It took the disciples some time, according to the New Testament, to make up their minds. Hallucinatory or real? Saul saw a vision on the road to Damascus. Hallucinatory or real? I mention these as you would know of them in your Church which, you say, never changes. I call them "inexplicable" but this does not mean that they should be treated as stopping points in all history.'

Christopher Columbus looked angry – 'Should I treat you as an "inexplicable" appearance? Not religious but artistic. Of course not. You are nothing but a visitor who comes to this huge canvas every evening and who has decided to masquerade as the man who was shot. What I am asking is this – how does he change, how does he die and live?'

I was worried suddenly, in an indefinable way, about the spectator (whom I now called Columbus) with whom I spoke. He was about fifty. He wore long hair that reached to his shoulders. He was dark, of mixed blood perhaps. He may have been Venezuelan or Spanish. His face was rather sharp, sharp nose, sharp lips. They dominated his features. But his eyes had a way of popping out of his head. I had seen this before. Yet, despite this eccentricity, they were kind, large, open, kindling. They were humorous, stubborn, proud. He looked around pleased that there was no one else in the room except ourselves. Perhaps, though he would not admit it, he enjoyed talking with me. No one else had shared his intense curiosity about the enormous canvas that encircled the walls and seemed curiously enough to reach into the City. This imaginary extension created a barrier between us though it revealed a hidden uncertainty in Columbus. I felt our conversation, however peculiar it seemed, must go on. More for his sake than for mine.

I spoke softly, placatingly, though why I should be placatory was beyond my judgement. 'You say your fascination rests, in part, on new things that appear in the canvas. Are those new things masquerades as well? Do things, that we assume to be passive, masquerade *in the canvas of history* – if I may use your words – and tell us something important we have forgotten even as they may mislead us and take us along the wrong path? We may restrict ourselves with each "inexplicable" appearance – religious or artistic – or we may open ourselves to explore a Darkness . . .'

He broke in. 'Ah! yes, you refer to Mind in Darkness. I have seen this in the painting. All myth!'

I was irritated by his blank dismissal of what I had said. 'Myth bears on the *two lives we both live*. I am quoting your remark! It bears as well on legend *and* reality, masquerade *and* the inexplicable, ancient *and* modern, life *and* death . . .'

He broke in again – 'How does this painting bring life and death together? Tell me!'

'It's everywhere, but you do not see it.'

He was obsessed. There was no doubt about it. His obsession led him to strive to make *his* Church an all-important feature in the New World. So all-important it ignored or suppressed all other faiths that sprang from primitivity, so-called, primitive fire, primitive tree, primitive water, primitive sky, primitive soil, primitive rock . . . There was something quite extraordinary in all this for it pointed to grave dangers that could affect him, dangers I could not define.

'Do you know', I said as softly as before, 'why primitive faiths are important? The primitives believe in a god of fire, a god of water, a god of the soil, a god of rivers . . . In this way they see – whether they perceive it logically or not – that *the psyche is dismembered* and may only be somewhat united again, in its parts, with and through Nature, through diversity.'

I hesitated for a moment, fearing I was becoming portentous, whereas I was seeking to enlighten someone fascinated by a work of Art he could not accept.

'In this way', I continued slowly, 'we begin to approach *the mystifying emergence of Man on this planet.*'

Columbus broke in so sharply he made me jump – '*Man is created in the image of God. What do primitives know?*'

My phantom limbs, under their concealing pebbled attire, were settling into solidity.

'The image of God', I ventured to say, 'is in itself a mystery.'

My tongue became numb. Perhaps his was too, for he did not reply. With an effort we gathered the shreds of our voices back together again. The effort was greater on my side than on his. How did I speak to him, how did I address him, with paint in my voice? His was the voice of history, stopping points of history he wished to impose on the canvas on the wall.

'One hundred million years ago (I am uncertain of the precision of numbers – it could be more, it could be less – it was in the Cretaceous period, anyway) the Dinosaurs lost their hold on planet Earth. You speak of the image of God . . .'

'A beautiful image, is it not?' He was pleading with me.

'Perhaps it is. Perhaps it is. I was about to remind you that the Dinosaurs strolled like giants through places where now are great Cathedrals (with images of God as *absolute* human vessels maimed or crucified) and great Cities. They governed the Earth for millions of years. Then a meteorite or meteoroid or whatever struck. Cataclysmic! The giants were seized. They died instantly. Not only they but the *majority* of animals living then. *We are related to every creature in the tree of life and death*! The shock, the blow, if I may judge from the Dream of Art, dismembered the psyche of Earth (if I may use such a term as "psyche" for the mystery of power and powerlessness that resides in all things). Primitive faith is a faint trace of the massive shock to rivers, to rocks, trees, to soil, to oceans, everything, to the Earth in itself. This is complex, I know, it challenges taking things, even the *shape of Man*, for granted . . .'

'*I do not believe in evolution.* I use "evolve" to indicate changes that are immediate, superficial you would say. And I do not accept "psyche" in the way you abuse it. The psyche of Earth! Totally absurd!' The peremptory tone of voice came again after the plea he had made. Were there two or three voices in the room?

'Superficialities may have deep roots, deeper than you imagine. So have absurdities. Who are our ancestors – among the animals that survived – after the cataclysm? Small mammalian creatures who had lived – concealed for much of the time – in the shadow of the giants. Did they know *pain*? *Pain is the mystery of the unconscious that breaks into consciousness.* Primitive faith is aware of this. It transfers human pain into trees, it shares human pain with the Earth. It drives a nail into a tree to relieve human suffering. A tree is apparently

34

unconscious. *The psyche of the Earth*! What is *pain*, a universe of *pain*? Do fish suffer with a hook in their mouth? Do birds suffer when they are shot? Does a butterfly feel its wings break when it is crushed in the palm of our hand? Does the living Earth groan in its arteries and veins?

'These questions may only be approached by an Art that brings Tricksters upon the floor of a gallery, or the floor of a world, the floor of history.

'*Was it an accident*? Was the cataclysmic blow the Earth received an accident? The Trickster tricks his way into Darkness and Light, the Darkness of Mind . . . What is Mind? What is universal Mind?

'Flowers appeared suddenly on the planet – in the wake of the cataclysm that seized so many – and they gave our ancestors fruit, honey, and energy. Darwin said of such flowers, appearing so suddenly, that they were an "abominable mystery". He could have said the same of the cataclysm that the Earth suffered.

'This gives the Artist today a supreme opportunity to create a spectre of Mind through Tricksters, through Prophets, through Lovers, through Beggars, through Wanderers . . . All will appear on the floor of history and will speak of the mystifying emergence of men and women, of their shape, which I cannot accept *psychically* as absolute. They are small, they are large, they are inexplicable, they are masqueraders, they are devilish, they are foolish, they are wise, they are nothing, they are something, they carry traces of desolation and of memory . . .

'What are the catastrophes, minor or major, that we endure but reminders of a violence which we need to transfigure and to share with all being that has suffered acutely in the past?

'To die into creativity is the theme of the man who falls into a painting with a wound he shares with all others whether they know it or not.'

There came voices approaching from a neighbouring room. Columbus swung away from me to see who it was. He did not have long to wait. Two men arrived at the door. They greeted him as they entered: 'Hello! Christopher. We heard you talking and we wondered whom you had met.'

'Hello! George and Andy. Good to see you again. Hope you enjoyed the Renaissance pieces at which you have been looking. I was speaking to . . .' He swung back towards me but I was no longer there. He was utterly astonished. 'He was here a moment ago. Where the devil has he gone?'

'Through *that* door,' said Andy. He was pointing to another door into a room leading to a corridor that took one into the street.

'Did you see him leave?'

'He left before we arrived. You may have scared him away, old chap!' He was laughing light-heartedly.

'A funny man he was,' said Columbus. 'Mad I would say. You would have been terribly surprised if you had seen him. He was dressed as the Trickster in the canvas. Pebbled dress. Painted lines on his face. Exactly! I have not seen him before. I forgot to ask his name. Trickster was the name I gave him. He comes in the evenings, he told me.' There was a far-away, slightly bewildered look in Columbus's eyes that had darkened.

'In the evenings! That is true. There is a curious bunch of chaps here in the evenings . . .'

'How do you know of this?'

'One of the people who run the gallery mentioned it to me,' said Andy. 'They are rehearsing a play based on this very painting.' They were all now staring at the canvas on the wall with its lines and threads that seemed to reach out and meet them.

'That's bad,' said Columbus. 'I am thinking of writing an article on this painting. It's a mass of tricks.'

'But you come so often to see it. I do not understand.'

'I have never told you why I am here. You are studying the Renaissance work and we meet and pass each other. I come to this painting because I know the territory that is painted. I

36

know how people may be seduced and may come to the wrong conclusions. I am for the Church, which is Light, and never changes. A play which looks elsewhere, into Darkness, is bad. The play should be stopped.'

'My dear chap, I never realised you were so dogmatic, so authoritarian. You have one view. That's fair enough. They have another. No one can say who is right. You may find yourself doing violence to secure your view. It happens all the time in the world in which we live.'

'I am right,' said Columbus. 'I know I am right.'

'Be careful,' said Andy, 'they may send you back to Castile in chains.' He began to smile as he spoke.

'In chains!' cried Columbus. He was taken aback. Then his lips curled into a smile. He saw the humour in Andy's remark. 'If I am, King Ferdinand and Queen Isabella will free me and restore me to a height.' He contemplated 'height' in the painting. The 'height' that Ferdinand and Isabella would restore to him gave him a sudden flashing sensation of a link between himself and the Trickster. They seemed different yet the flash of a 'height' that no one could fathom made him sensitive to a ghost of memory he saw in the painting.

'What did the Trickster say that disturbed you so greatly that you feel the play should be abandoned?'

Columbus became nonchalant to conceal the flash of 'height' that had bewildered him. 'Oh!' he said, 'I know it all. He spoke what I knew. But I left it to him to pretend he was telling me what I did not know. I wanted to change him and me *at a blow*. I wanted to bring him into the Church, to stop him from entering a Darkness I saw in myself as well. Religion is inimitable in this way. It throws a net over those who seem to be utterly opposed to each other. Some call this an absolute doctrine or dictatorship. But it is the only *right*. I intended saying this to him but he left so suddenly I was unable to do so. Perhaps he did not want you to see him.'

George, the younger of the two men, who was about forty, with a slight drizzle of hair on his cheeks, turned from the canvas and faced Columbus. He began to speak rather diffidently – 'I do not agree with you, Chris,' he said. 'Perhaps – who knows? – the Trickster may have felt that the unity of opposites you suggest is a fallacy, except both sides see each other differently, with open minds.' He paused then continued: 'Your unity is based on a violent blow which one side delivers to the other. Surreptitiously perhaps. Not necessarily physically. Though physicality can happen.'

'A fallacy?' Columbus exclaimed. 'What do you mean?'

'I mean that no one can ever be absolutely right. Rightness, yes, is within us, but what we think we know of ourselves and others is *tainted*. All knowledge is tainted by the sensation that one knows absolutely what the other thinks, that they both see with an unchanging light. Who governs that light if not one or the other? There is great danger here. We may have moments, flashes, that are inimitably the same, that bring us together in a community of being I would think we have lost. Perhaps that's what this painting is all about. I do not know. If it is – is this not true humility? There may be a Darkness that we need to enter.'

3

I had now come to a crucial moment in my journey along the River and the Forest. The Sky was painted with speckled darts as though predicting a mood of violence not entirely, however, of 'abominable mystery', as had occurred in the Age of the Dinosaurs. I felt it was possible to draw from such darts or strokes a frail thread of an element of truth that led into possibilities other than sheer violence. Would this thread bring, I wondered, a new, uncertain light into the mystifying emergence of Man on planet Earth?

Two darts or strikes were particularly ominous in the painting. One sprang from the hand of the Titan. The other came from the speckled skeleton of a goddess in a constellation far away in the painted Skies.

The Titan's hand was pointing at me. My night-eyes were disabled but they could see his lined, painted fingers holding a shaft that was aimed at me. For whom was the dart from the goddess intended? My night-eyes gave me a clue. I searched the canvas as though it disclosed portions of the hidden Mind of the universe. I searched for someone with disabled night-eyes like mine, blind yet mysteriously seeing. In a flash, out of the painted Sky, I perceived Tiresias, seer and prophet. He was the only figure in distant cultures I felt was possessed of night-eyes resembling mine.

Tiresias and I became a cross-cultural masquerade, in a cross-cultural psychical dress, Prophet and Beggar.

Illusion and presence? The canvas was so interwoven with lines it was impossible to tell where illusion lay, where presence lay.

I myself had been painted in lines on the canvas of space. Tiresias had emerged from a great distance as though his culture existed in the Skies rather than on Earth. Was this a sign of dismembered psyche? It touched our imaginations with mystery that brought Sky and Earth closer together than the Titan wished them to be as though he wanted psyche and imagination to remain broken, in separate compartments, without a perception in humanity of disablements in itself.

We – Tiresias and I – were now embarked on an immense journey in the hidden Mind of Art. Yes, I had been painted in lines on the canvas. How illusory were those lines, how real? How illusory were the closeness and the distance in the figure of Tiresias, how real? Were we now psychically linked together, did we now share the same paradoxes, disablements that we perceived as real, so real, they led us to search for new, perhaps painful ways of overcoming them?

The lines that were my body on the canvas reached to Tiresias. I felt we were close where Sky and Earth formed a delicate, *quantum* room of light that we fired in explosive radiance in response to the blow we would receive or had already received *in the void of space and time.*

Had we foiled the blow? The light we fired was frail, it broke into action and counter-action making room for change, it made a hollow, meaningful intersection within the dart or spear of violence. We saw ourselves differently, we saw ourselves slightly beyond our lined bodies in the painting, making room to break the stroke of violence. The blow the Titan and the goddess delivered entered that room of *dissolving powers* ... We had fires of reflection – however disabled we seemed – on our enemies who are helpless (though they may not realise it) in their lust for direct, unassailable action that they gain (as they see it) from their mythological parents, the Titan and the goddess, who insinuate themselves into material nature until they become utterly real ...

Tiresias and I felt we knew the difference between illusion and presence – in the room that quantum action and counter-action brought to us, in the light of the void in the hidden Mind of Art – but the blend of lines, reaching from Earth to Sky, made us aware of our weakness of psyche in drawing them apart. We wondered if our muscularity of the imagination was strong enough for us to climb heights, descend into depths, in search of precarious presences in painted space. Yet the subtle differences between us gave us strengths we did not possess as totally separate beings in totally separate cultures. I felt I walked on painted land, on painted water, in painted air. Had I abandoned the ruses of the Trickster? How could I when I walked on paint? Paint stood above and beneath reality and in that room lay the mystery of Mind. What is truth? An old question posed by hypocrites in the past but a new question, in all seriousness, posed by Art. My night-eyes were engaged with the eyes of Tiresias, blind yet mysteriously seeing. Prophet and Beggar.

The River ran smooth as a pavement in a City, the roaring rapids I had left behind were the dull thunder of machines that seemed to be as much in a future, ahead of me, as in a past, behind me.

Tiresias prophesied we were coming to a City buried in the soil. We would need to descend as Odysseus had done when he met the shadow of his mother and of the warriors he knew at Troy. They were little suns in the darkness of space that had to be fed with blood to gain a reflection of life. The Arawaks wore no ideal dress. They too were akin to shadows of presence on the stage of death and life. They had seen pyramids in ancient America from which hearts had tumbled like animals of the Brain and the Sun. They decided not to wear the robe of the priests nor the garment of the victims, privileged or otherwise.

'The City was flooded,' I said to Tiresias. 'See the watermark on the trees. A very high flood-mark! It caused desolation I have no doubt and everyone who lived here must have fled into the Forest. It happened a long time ago. How do the Arawaks know of this?'

'Olmec City,' said Tiresias. 'The Arawaks have passed here before. This is a new lot of their people. They have been coming in groups for generations. This is the last lot.'

I was astonished. 'How do you know of this?' I asked.

'I see it in a void of time in the painting in which we walk,' said Tiresias. 'What happened yesterday happens today and makes us weep. Such is the art of prophecy. Looking back, looking forward. Looking through a complacent humanity into the ways it repeats itself without knowing it does so.'

'You come from Thebes,' I said. 'How do you know of Olmec City? The Olmec sculpture from which the City is named is amongst the earliest works of Art in ancient America. It is huge, a giant head, no body, no feet. No one knows how it was quarried from stone that exists far away from where it now rests and carried across a maze of land and water.'

'I see Olmec City in a Cloud that passes with tear-drops. How do you know of Odysseus? You see him in a blood-drop. Each drop, tear or blood, is a flood we cannot easily measure. Where do floods come from? They come from the heart of the universe that speaks to us – whether we hear it or not – and spreads itself in the Skies above and in the ground beneath. I see it in *you*. We are close together, are we not? I see it in your unconscious that speaks to me wordlessly in the spirit of your hands that touch me, in signs that flutter like wings. I appear blind. My eyes are open to consciousness and unconsciousness. Your eyes are open to Thebes, which is raised into the Clouds. It is no longer there as it was. Yet it is there in the breaking fabric of the universe that re-shapes itself invisibly and visibly into a room, a lighted place. Such is the art of ghosts of memory.'

I was astonished at Tiresias's sayings. His night-eyes were everywhere, in sounds, in sights, in the wings of a bird, in visibility and invisibility.

'I am a ghost of memory,' I exclaimed. 'Does this mean that I live in consciousness and unconsciousness? Consciousness fades. The unconscious remains, untapped, unspoken for. Is this how I should see *you* and *myself*? Are you my *speaking* unconscious, speaking in me, and through me, come to the surface at last? Perhaps it's always been there but I never felt it so vividly before.'

'You are my *listening* conscious realm. It's always been there though it is suppressed and forgotten with many who do not realise the part they play. When we are divided we lose the chance to know the sorrows and perils of Mankind. We do not dominate each other. We mourn with each other. Mourning is not understood. People say they are happy even though they mourn unconsciously. Olmec City is the City of mourning.'

We came to Olmec City at last. Before I knew where I was I fell through an unexpected hole in the pavement or smooth, painted River into a lighted room which was a white silvery mix, bright, beautiful but ominous in a way I did not immediately see. Nor did I see the smooth, painted water – painted by Nature – running beneath the surface of the Earth on which I walked so easily. The Arawaks were aware of this. They worshipped – amongst their gods – a god of volcanoes that left holes in the pavements of Cities as a warning of the mystery of place. I looked around and saw a large bowl in the middle of the floor.

Everything had an air of superb originality as an omen of beauty which disguises the relationship between surfaces and depths. Had I descended or arisen when I fell into Earth and Sky? My lined body rose from the ground where it had been lying when it fell. It all happened with a spontaneity that left me bewildered and confused. I looked up and saw Tiresias descending on a ladder and his night-eyes shone within mine, it seemed, as though he came from beneath above. He was looking at me with his veiled sight, the veils were peculiar.

They fell upon me like a Beggar's ragged cloak. The bowl in the middle of the floor settled and I was struck by its appearance. It was of Olmec design, it was large. It had opened to reveal an infant-Child lying like flesh and stone within it: flesh painted in lines of growing stone, stone as vulnerable flesh. It was strangely alive as though it was destined to remain a Child to the end of time.

Tiresias's night-eyes, that seemed my own, peered into every corner of the room as if they found something there that was distant, in veiled sight, yet as close as my finger-tips lit now – not by the Titan but by Tiresias's hidden fires in shining water and breaking Cloud.

All at once I had come closer to the bowl in the middle of the floor. The bowl was a giant Olmec head, miniaturised to imply great proportions, carefully sliced to make a bed for the infant-Child lying within it. *There it was! A Child and also a Brain – fashioned to appear veined and tender as a Child – so intertwined infancy and old age came together at this moment.* I remembered the uncanny skill with which the huge, sculptured head had appeared to supervise its movement, ages ago, across a maze of lands and waters. No one knew for certain how it was done.

A feat of the Brain that may have turned so complacent, it relied on technologies to take over its material achievements. Was the Olmec head halfway already between veined, human flesh and stony technology? Except for the Infant perhaps, *an Infant of hope*, sleeping now in its ancestral cradle, sleeping helplessly, in need of the greatest care and attention, within its early years (that seemed centuries) to live, to survive.

The human Brain had leapt, from brutal small-globed forebears, within a rapid, *geological* span of time – akin to a void over millions of years when suns rose and set and no one knew which was which.

Did the human Brain leap and evolve, over those millennia, in compensation for a growing reduction in animal instincts? It still carries the nerve-end of those instincts. It lacks the protective fur of the animal. Its skull is thin. It maintains an extended Childhood, full of ambivalences and fears, into immature maturity, and into old age. The price of a large, globular Brain that becomes the dominant Sun of the body (and of bodilessness) and confuses narrow self-protective ruses for the hidden Mind of love.

I turned to Tiresias and I confided in him. Then I asked him a question which surprised him.

'This is the City of mourning,' I said. 'What does one mean by narrow self-protection? But above all do you think that there is any hope for Mankind in the Infant painted like a tender, young Brain of the future?'

Tiresias was silent for a long while then he replied: 'I am something of a wanderer as well as a prophet. I have left Thebes and visited some of the greatest modern poets. But I sense that Man may have leapt by evolution into his calculating, psychological Brain but he is, as you put it, in a state of extended Childhood. He is acutely vulnerable. No wonder he *feels* that his family, his ethnic ancestors, come first. He *feels* this, he (or she) *feels* this to be true. Until he can make another leap from Childhood into virtually impossible maturity he will continue to clothe his vulnerability with Childhood fantasies of parochial rightness, parochial narrowness. He stands on a border-line between the animal and the divine, the animal Child and the divine possibility of a true maturity. This is hope in the City of mourning.'

I could not tell whether the room had darkened in the canvas of space or whether we moved invisibly and were still lines of paint. (We contemplated the painting from without as I had done with Christopher Columbus. I hid my phantom limbs from him. I appeared to be solid.) Or whether Tiresias and I and the Arawaks had descended into another chamber. It was dark now. There were patches of clay on the walls. The clay seemed daubed there by the flood, daubed and painted by Nature. This was much more in keeping with a recollection of the flood than the lighted room had been. Yet – even as I felt so – I was uncertain. Light could have many purposes in a canvas in which one knew oneself within and without, without spiritually, within materially in painted lines. One perceived oneself again across generations and centuries. Did not Tiresias arrive from within a place which was known to have existed centuries before Christ?

Whatever I knew (or thought I knew) I was ignorant of the complex universe of Art in which I moved from the present into the past, from the past into the present.

The Arawaks resembled the people who had fled from the City when the great flood came. They were without the canvas and still within it.

I had confessed to my ignorance when I claimed – but a moment or two ago – that Nature was the painter who daubed the walls with clay. The painter used elements drawn from Nature (this was true) to imply the return of the people who had fled into the Forest. Perhaps – in his artistry – he saw Tiresias and me as spiritual instruments, natural instruments, to record the strangeness of his vision.

Were not plays the business of Nature? Was not theatre the business of spirit? One records a play so that it is always there and can be seen at the time of the recording and years after on a screen. Reality becomes a cinematic spirit by which one lives in the past – without questioning what one sees – as though the present and the past are capable of being combined in a moment. Take this away and humanity would feel bereft. Yet few, if any, see this as a void in space and time through spirit.

Art links all of these mythological suppositions and seeks a deeper meaning which may be insoluble. Spirit is the business of Art. Art composes the play of the grave, the universal grave of Mankind and goes a step or two across centuries and beyond every dissolving or dissolved body which is in ashes.

Tiresias sees the spirit of Art in this very dark but bright light. His eyes are blind yet mysteriously seeing. He sees ghosts of memory returning in the nakedness of the Arawaks, a spiritual nakedness, reflected in the Sky above the City, in Cloud-shapes opening nevertheless like rags. One glimpses their spirit through every ragged Cloud. They are playing in painted Cloud and Sky that they are the people returning to the City. An extraordinary play. Spirit is invisible however real it may seem to be. Tiresias sees it in a play of fragment upon fragment, in his blind/seeing eyes, rag upon rag, *disclosing an incalculable shape* beneath, within/without a Cloud. Spirit stands outside as well as within the canvas of space painted by the Artist like a Cloud. Furthermore, on the other hand, the players in this game of spirit were equally reflected in mirroring waters on Earth rising into space and into heavy rainfall that flooded a City. Thus each player presented himself or herself as a member of the people in a creature of the flood, incalculable in the Sky, descending on Earth. This was the dance of Sky and Earth in the City of mourning the Artist sought to paint.

Tiresias and I followed the Arawaks into the clay-daubed theatre of the City. Not only clay but wood and iron at a window which was cleverly placed so as not to distract attention from the painting on the walls. It was dark but flashes of lightning shone in the painted Clouds on the canvas of space, they shone, they flashed, they were fires of the phallus from the mouth of the Olmec giant. They melted swiftly, they shone swiftly, bringing the thunder of the rapids in their wake. A threatening storm. Was this a prelude to the flood or did it bring memories of heavy rainfall in every City, ancient or modern?

'What does all this mean?' I demanded of Tiresias. He was the one who knew, I felt.

'It means that the monumental head of the Olmec giant is painted in a lightning Cloud, a lightning storm, flashing in phallic lines through the giant's mouth. No one sees this often. Or if they do they pay no attention to what they mean.'

'I do not understand,' I said softly. 'What do the phallic lines imply?'

Tiresias considered the matter closely and then he replied: 'Let me interpret what I can from the play which takes place in the City. Each creature of the flood has something to say implicitly about the giant Olmec.' He looked around at the

47

environment of the City, which was partly hidden from us by the walls of the gallery on which the painting stood though they seemed sometimes to be within the painting. We heard the roar of the City, ghost-cars running in the rapids, a plane. There was a curious, sudden clip-clop of a woman in high-heeled shoes walking in the Street. Our attention was fixed on her from amongst the Arawaks. She was a creature of the flood returning to the City.

'Do the fires apply to her and to all Mankind?' I asked again.

Tiresias said: 'As you see, the players – let us call them the people – built a wooden body and legs to uphold the head of the giant. It happens in different forms everywhere. Sometimes a warrior's head, sometimes a politician's . . . The fires come from the mouth. They burn their way into the lower organs. Everything turns to ashes. Only the head remains.'

Tiresias's eyes were fixed on the walls as though they saw through clay and water and air, and everything blocking a universal view, with each lightning flash that outlined the creature of the flood we had heard walking on the Street.

I saw it all clearly now. I saw the giant's head. Eyes, nose, lips, gaze, all in one tigerish intensity like the blow of a monument. They were not sliced into a bed for an Infant I had seen in another room.

I wished now to find the creature of the flood we had heard arriving in the Street, in the rapids.

'Where is she?' I cried. 'Where is she? Will she vanish like the sound of water playing clip-clop on a rock?'

Tiresias looked at me with his seeing/blind eyes. His lips moved: 'Will *you* vanish? You are both without, within this painted room. You have your parts to play. Surely you know that the play in every people (whether they are conscious of it or not) is about *spirit* and *materiality*. In a creature of the flood you have to make a distinction to bring the painting alive. Have you not been doing so in blundering ways all

48

along? You have to do it again and again. There is material tragedy, there is spiritual entity. Can you see what is the difference? The phallic fires descend from the mouth of the giant above the rapids – the thunder of the rapids – and bring *castration*, yes, *castration*. It is called *oral* castration. Sex is ashes.'

I became angry. 'Sex is *not* ashes. People live through sex . . .'

'When I say oral castration I am saying something more than physical impotence. A giant may possess all his limbs and still be spiritually impotent. He may perform the act of sex like a ghost in the rapids of history which give voice to insensible machineries. He is himself the ghost of such machinery, sexual machinery.'

I was so driven by Tiresias's remarks that I stepped out of the canvas into the gallery, hid myself partially behind a large table and chairs, and listened for the sound of the creature of the flood I had heard walking in the rapids of the Street. Her voice rippled up from below and all I could make out were three words: 'O . . . my . . . God . . .' There followed a brutal, male, vituperative voice which seemed to be ordering her to kneel or to cringe.

'O my God,' I repeated. 'What is he saying to her?'

Christopher Columbus turned to me. He stared at me, seeing me for the first time – 'You came into the gallery quite suddenly. I did not see you arrive. You are obviously one of those fool-players playing the Art of the City. Everything's taken from this painting! I shall stop that play. It is outrageous. Look how you are dressed in rags like a Beggar. I see the Beggar in the canvas. You hide much of yourself from me behind that big table and chairs. But I see your painted face and hands. You look exactly like the Beggar in the canvas. Let me tell you one thing straightaway! The woman you hear below in the Street is a prostitute . . .'

'No, she is not. She is a creature of the flood. She is an Arawak.'

49

Christopher Columbus began to laugh. 'Every brown-faced woman is an Arawak. You are quite mad. Creature of the flood! What does it mean? Tell me! I see it in the canvas. But what does it mean?'

'It means', I said, trying to placate him, 'that she has experienced a disastrous flood in her village in South America, which is rumoured to stand on the path to a lost City. She is haunted by the heavy rainfall that she knew. This City – modern as it is – is panelled with the ruin of Cities which have been flooded or fired or desolated. You may not see those panels. She does. Who is the brute that pursues her? This is a reasonably quiet corner of the Street though I hear cars. Why can't they stop and help her? He may kill her. I shall call the police.' I hesitated, knowing that if I stepped out from behind the table and the chairs to reach a telephone I would expose my phantom limbs.

Columbus stood close to the window. 'The man has gone,' he said at last, 'she is alone down there. No point in ringing for the police. She should go to a Church and confess to her sins.' He turned from the window towards me – 'You are the Beggar! I see you are dressed exactly as in the painting. Where is your companion the Prophet Tiresias? It's all there in the painting, which I visit frequently and find so outrageous. I shall put a stop to the play you take from this canvas and are rehearsing in the evenings when I'm not here. Who are you? The Tiresias in the canvas is a fraud.'

I was shocked by his prejudice, his bigotry, as it seemed to me. 'Do not bother about me,' I said. 'You will learn who I am in due course. As for Tiresias, I thought you would have learnt he helps us to see the painting differently from within and from without, to consider afresh what we thought we knew absolutely. Even in ancient Thebes Tiresias had a core-value no one fully understood. He was blind/seeing then and punished by a goddess. We need to see that punishment differently. It is as much in ourselves, as in our ignorance of what lies beyond ourselves, as in a goddess. We need to see "seeing" and "blindness" differently. Tiresias changes – as we all do – his/our fragmentary appearance across the centuries . . . There is an indefinable spirit within those fragments – put it as you like – with which, through which, we make new fictions, new plays . . .'

'Nonsense,' said Columbus. 'Have you read Dante's *The Divine Comedy*? Dante is a very great poet . . .'

'No, I have not read it.'

'There you will find that Homer and Virgil and all who belong to pre-Christian ages can go no further than a sphere called Purgatory. Their core – as you put it – is fixed. It is unalterable. Fictions and plays are heavily influenced by this notion though writers may not realise it.'

I was astonished. 'I cannot believe that,' I said. 'No further than a sphere laid down by a poet? Infinity – if it exists – is barred from them? A dictatorial world beneath the surfaces of freedom . . .'

'Nothing dictatorial there. It's the divinity of my Church. You are a heretic. Your play is rank heresy.'

I felt it was my turn to laugh but my laughter rolled hollow in the rapids of history. I pulled myself together. 'Do you not think', I said, 'that your Church does the same thing – in some degree anyway – as this painting is suggesting?'

'How so?'

'The disciples of Christ stand, I would think, on a borderline. Are they pre-Christian? I do not know. They lived before your Church had come into play. Mary, the mother, is now called the Mother of God. Is this not a special translation, so to speak, of Mary, the mother of Jesus?'

'Stop! Stop! Divinity cannot be translated. I see the entrance of the divine into history as unalterable.'

'Are you not actually playing with an indefinable spirit? How can you restrict this to your faith alone? How can you throw millions and millions of men and women into a prison because they come from outside the entrance of the divine – as you determine when this is – into history? Dante may be a very great poet but he is limited.'

'Limited! *You* are the one who is limited.'

'Yes, I know I am. That is why I seek new shapes – not just for their novelty but as a way of approaching what is insoluble yet may be real. The approach of an open Mind which evolves – if I may so put it – through fragments, through shifts, in the stream of time.'

'I tell you I shall stop this play before it is performed. Heresy! You tamper with evil and good. You do not see there is absolute evil, absolute good.'

'I do not see absolutes,' I confessed. 'I am a limited apparition in the canvas of space. Absolutes, I feel, reinforce partialities until they conceal them from view. This has helped to promote genocides, holocausts. It promotes terrifying divides *we cannot see* between the conscious, the subconscious, the unconscious, between Brain and the Mind of love.'

Columbus became violently angry. He stormed out of the gallery and left me alone. It was late afternoon. Shadows were gathering everywhere. I moved closer to the window. The Arawak woman held herself now against a monument in a park beside the Street. She clutched it in anguish. I saw her waist and breasts in the shape of a violin. Her head and feet were hidden from me in a deep, ashen shadow that lay upon one side of the monument. Or she may have placed herself halfway in a clutch or opening in the monument.

4

Had I left Tiresias – without his knowing it – in the room into which we had followed the Arawaks? Perhaps I had been away but for a moment or two. He had not seen me go. He was blind to my return. How could I explain this in his 'seeing' through his 'blindness'?

He seemed to know nothing of my voyage into a stormy meeting with Christopher Columbus. And yet I knew he was a great seer. He was omniscient.

A moment, I felt, in the life of a seer – the moment of my leaving the room and returning to the room – is an eternity, yet it passes away like the flicker of a candle. *This gave me a clue.*

Such a flicker is more than a flicker when measured across the abyss of life and death. It tells of the *eye* that sees our crowded, historical encounters which seem to last for ever even as we are blind – as a stroke or fixture of paint – to the swiftness of their passing. The seer's blindness becomes a universal paradox. History is blind though we lean on it as though it knows everything.

I was stricken by what I felt. An unconscious function in myself had broken through my rational surface sensibilities to bring the seer more challengingly alive than I thought I knew. May I not have learnt something invaluable from the flicker of a candle in his 'seeing blindness'?

Tiresias had not seen me go, he had not seen me return. Was he not omniscient?

What is omniscience in the Mind of a god or a seer or a prophet? Is it a field of images which stirs the memory of

Man beyond material codes of 'knowing' or 'seeing'? I may remember things I did with one side of myself unknown to the other side. Is there a 'memory' through and beyond one's 'broken-ness'?

Such images may in themselves awaken me to my 'broken-ness'. The seer's consciousness and unconsciousness are an invaluable clue.

I was broken into two when Christopher Columbus left me in the gallery in anger at the words I had spoken.

One half of me thought of a god who knew everything and I remembered Tiresias's sight and sightlessness . . . The other half of me was dazzled into flickering activity beyond sight and sightlessness.

I was awakening Man arisen from the unconscious . . . It was late afternoon. The sun cast its shadows in the rags of cloud on the monument or rock in the rapids of the City. *I saw now what I had not seen then.* Those rags were Man's awakening. *I* had extended myself into the rapids and into the Arawak woman upon a rock. *I* would rescue her. A moment's extension, the flicker of a candle in the eye of Imagination . . .

I had not seen myself go there. *I* had not seen myself return from the monument or the rock in the rags of a Beggar. But *I* had been there and had returned in the flicker of an eye.

The flicker is more than a flicker. It brings the involuntary shadowy visions of a god or a seer into Man's non-seeing excursions across an abyss of cruelty and love.

'*Who am I?* What am *I?* What is Man?' I demanded of Tiresias. 'You have prompted me to see myself as a hero. You have prompted me to discern differences between memory (as an active creative force) and remembrance (as a passive acceptance of history). Man becomes a hero in your promptings. Is this not the City of mourning? You have said it is. Does this not make Man into a devil as much as a hero, into a priest as much as a murderer? He worships saints and kills those he calls witches. What and who is Man? Who am *I?* What am *I?*'

Tiresias was startled. 'I prompted you?' he asked softly almost under his breath. 'I did not know . . .'

'You are omniscient,' I cried. 'Your shadow revives the sleeping memory of Man.'

Tiresias looked even more startled. 'Omniscience', he said at last, 'is only possible with the gods.' He considered the issue of 'the gods'. I felt his reflections moving in the canvas of space. Are there gods of the unconscious *and* of the conscious?

'Look at the Arawaks,' he said suddenly. 'They carry the sculpture of a woman who is headless, limbless, and whose remaining body in their hands is violin-shaped and beautiful. They worship her as a goddess. Can she (the goddess) say whether she has been sculpted as a form of cruelty or love? Has cruelty lines of beauty?'

I did not reply. But I was struck by my memory of the violin-shaped body of the Arawak woman I had seen upon the monument or rock in the rapids of the City. A dark shadow had sliced her head and limbs away from her and left music, the music in the body of a goddess. Did the violin sing of cruelty or of love? It carried the echoes of abysses between planet and planet, galaxy and galaxy. (Who knows what forms life may take in distant galaxies?) Perhaps a part of me knew, the other part didn't.

'She is Cycladic,' Tiresias continued, 'and she closely resembles an Arawak sculpture that is limbless, with a musical body, and a smooth face, so smooth it looks like a constellation falling from heaven . . .'

I felt uneasy at what seemed an exaggeration of likenesses and I interrupted by asking, 'What is Cycladic?'

'Ancient Greek,' Tiresias replied. '3000 BC. Three thousand years before Christ!'

'How could the Arawaks know of her?'

'The Arawak sculpture closely resembles the enterprise of the Greeks with their goddess . . .'

'Enterprise!' I cried. 'A cruel enterprise. Headless, limbless . . .'

55

'You forget how *broken* you yourself are. Such a breakage means the possibility of a new start, a new knowledge inscribed within sculptures, paintings, writings.' He stopped and considered, I felt, involuntary shadows, involuntary goddesses, in the beginning of the universe. 'It means', he continued, 'the energy to see and hear tunes that are radically different from *your* orchestration of surface sensibilities. You have a memory of such "newness" but it fades . . .'

He hesitated for a long while; and then he said slowly: 'Religion has an ancient origin which we cannot determine. You speak of promptings you got from me. So it is I learn from you about myself, you from me. And cultures learn from each other but no one knows how this happens. I have come a long way to find you. I am not the same figure that I was in the past. How could I be? I am in a Void of times, a painted Void. I am Tiresias of the Void. That is how I speak to you and how you hear me.' He stopped and waited for me to say something. But I was silent. *I knew of the Void – I had seen it before – but now that I perceived it entering into Tiresias – in ways I had not felt before – I felt I stood within new modes of past and present histories moving into undreamt-of futures.*

Tiresias spoke again – almost absent-mindedly – as though he were in the past and in the present: 'Do you not think these sculptures, Cycladic and Arawak, may warn us of fragments that could be interpreted as material cruelty or immaterial love? As love they belong to the future – to an unnameable future – and they seek to open our minds within and beyond illusions of constant form in a universe of which we know very little; they seek also to take us beyond the fear of absolute Darkness that has plagued humanity for ages.'

'Did the Arawaks go to Greece, or did the Greeks come to South America, in 3000 BC?' I spoke, in my broken condition, with a vein of self-mockery. I mocked myself as I mocked the Arawaks and the Greeks.

Tiresias looked through me, beyond me. 'It is possible,' he replied wryly. 'Anything is possible when extensions of unnameable spirit reach from age to age and influence the arts of the world. Who can say where that influence comes from? Is it involuntary? We do not give ourselves much of a chance to know the nature of a universe of "knowing" beyond what we think we know.'

I felt curiously ashamed in myself of myself. Had I not seen links between modern Giacometti and ancient Arawak sculptures? I had seen them but they had not aroused me to a broken-ness of self, encompassing two selves half-forgetful one of the other. Yet a new creativity may bring them into profound dialogue.

Tiresias suddenly spoke with some urgency. The Void had entered into him and I wondered what was afoot. I felt uncertain of the present and the future.

'You will now return to the River bank,' he said almost abruptly. 'You will not have far to go before coming to another room in this ancient City. Everything is in ruins. But not entirely. It is called a mourning City. I would say it is eternal, an eternal City . . .' He had become sombre, it seemed, as he spoke. 'There are parts to be found everywhere, the size of a room, the lights, electric or otherwise, the shape of a wall, the streets that run like threads in a canvas. And the insidious natures of cruelty and what passes for love. Remember this! There's treachery and there's subtlety.' He stopped for a moment, meditating, I felt, on modern Cities, which to him, coming from Thebes, were 'ruined' and 'ancient'. He had spoken of, or implied, 'undreamt-of futures' but now he saw deep into the ancient form of all things, the ancient spaces that cloaked all buildings.

'When you get to the room you will come upon the Wanderer and the Lovers. Listen to what the Wanderer tells you. *The fate of the Arawaks will depend on the Lovers.*'

This surprised me. But I said nothing. He continued: 'When I say the "fate of the Arawaks" I mean the "fate of the New World"! What is the New World but a strange alliance between new and old systems? The Arawaks are gentle. They need a form of "lightning courage" in their gentleness. "Lightning courage" brings Old World myths and habits – which must also change radically – into *light* gentleness.

'The Lovers are equipped – so the Wanderer will tell you – to achieve this. A woman of primitive Arawak craft, who is steeped in the ruses of Nature, must help a man of heroic myth. The help she gives him will lead to their marriage. It is not easy. They are equipped – the Wanderer will tell you – but you will see how difficult it is.' He hesitated for a moment before continuing: 'You are aware, I take it, that the Arawaks have a god of volcanoes . . .?'

'This is surprising. They are gentle, are they not?'

'Yes, they are. Gentle people worship fierce gods. It is a way of seeing the flaws in absolute gentleness. It is a way of opening themselves to constellations that fall to the earth. The god of volcanoes shoots terrible, skeleton stars into the sky. Stars or lights! A primitive people, however accomplished in their arts, see such lights as pointing to a greater Art which includes the Mind of love they have known all along as a Darkness. The volcanic stars that point into the skies hang back on the earth, come back close to the earth, and turn into a god. This is Nature's way of saying that the time has come for different worlds to meet and marry. It is not easy. But they may learn . . .'

'Learn what?'

Tiresias hesitated once again. His eyes flickered within the Void of space. 'They may learn that the darts of the volcano are not a pure sign of their betrayal (if this happens to them) by an absolute earth or an absolute sky. The passions of earth and of the sky are reflected mysteriously in the Lovers who may falsify their vows and bring about an explosive relationship between two worlds, the world of gentleness and the world of dogma. I speak as a dreamer. My dream may be awry and difficult to interpret. But this is the best I can do.'

He turned and made his way into a darkness in space and disappeared. His coat remained hanging on a wall. I was left disjointed, broken, and unable to believe he had gone.

I stepped out of the canvas. Christopher Columbus was not there. But George and Andy were looking at the great painting in the room I knew so well. *I stood beside them. They did not see me.* I was invisible. I wanted them to see me – as Columbus had done – and to speak to me as a player in the drama *Art of the City.* They knew the play was being rehearsed in the evenings and sometimes one or two players would come up in the gallery during the day to study the canvas on the wall. They would recognise me as a player. Or was I being played or acted and capable therefore of dramatic speech – however silent – to those who would listen? The rags of the Beggar which I wore concealed my limbs beautifully.

Was this the Void Tiresias had followed when he disappeared? Was this the Void that enters every great actor in a play when he dies on the stage and brings tears to the eyes of those who see him die? Do they weep for the actor or for the character he plays? Do they weep for themselves? Yet they arise and move out of the theatre and soon they forget the confines of Art – a painting, a play, whatever – that imprisons and releases simultaneously.

I looked at George and Andy and wondered whether in my absence/presence – invisibility beside them, visibility in the painting – I could convey to them something of this mystery.

I spoke to George silently. Christopher Columbus was away today. George was staring intently at the ragged Beggar in the painting. My voice came to him from nowhere, it seemed, and influenced his thoughts. He said to Andy: 'It grieves me when I find humanity so pathetic. What other word could I use? *Pathos* is the best term I know of. The pathos of humanity! Listen to the roar, it's in the voice of the rapids, it's muted, almost silent, but it falls like rain, it comes gently falling on the roof of the building. I hear it softly and distinctly when I listen to the rapids running beside the Beggar. The voice of the rapids in the City! The voice of the Beggar too. Don't laugh, Andy. I know it's absurd but that's how I feel. Not always. Sometimes. People are roaring their applause in the stadium and their voices come faintly in the distance but distinctly. It's pathetic. Yet it's quite extraordinary. Such muteness, such faintness, yet so *distinct*. One would swear the rapids in this painting are in the City. Is it something to do with the inner/outer strokes of the brush that run like falling, soundless/sounding water?'

'It depends on which way the wind is blowing,' said Andy in practicality. 'I must say, George, Christopher holds you in his spell. His acute and disturbed senses compel you to see the painting as he does.'

'No, no, not at all. I agree his disturbance has drawn me to *listen* more closely than I would have done otherwise. But I have an open mind to the strangest particulars whereas he condemns what he learns.'

George considered his feelings about Columbus. He liked him particularly for his sense of humour, in which he appeared to laugh at himself but which also exercised a blockage against a deeper knowing self that tended to be buried within stopping points in history. He added: 'It's much more than the way the wind blows, Andy . . .'

Andy brushed this aside and asked: 'What stadium are you thinking of?'

'The sports stadium, of course,' said George. 'An important boxing match is taking place there today. I thought you would know. The champion is fighting to defend his title.'

'Yes, I do know. You are quite right.'

'Have you been in the great Bush in South America?'

'No, I have not. Why do you ask?'

'The faint, distinct roar of voices in the stadium reminds me of the rapids in a great South American river which brings an uncanny, indescribable music to one's ears.' He stared at the Beggar, who was speaking to him dramatically but silently like a character in a book. 'I was something of a beggar there myself in those days. Little or no money but I managed to get around. I was a wanderer. Those rapids are not *described* in this painting, they are *in* the painting, so much that they become curiously relevant to all Cities, all cultures. They can be felt through Art in every City, every culture. This is an unconscious medium that is universal though we may hear it, see it, without knowing what we hear or see.

'You hear a variety of sounds in the rapids that are vague, in a sense, but vivid in the mind – horses' hooves running on a road, the swish and rush of cars, *and* the roar of crowds from far away arising distinctly like rain that cannot be mistaken . . . or sounding like veins of thin fire so far away in the leaves of trees blown by the wind they become more real than rain. The sound of rain becomes fire. It's here in this painting, Art and Nature combined mysteriously into a perception within us . . . Forgive me for being a trifle poetic. The magic in this painting brings me close, once again, to Venezuela, the Orinoco and Amazon rivers, the South American rainforests which I visited years ago . . .'

I, the Beggar, spoke to him and he listened.

'You have strayed far from the pathos of humanity of which you were speaking,' said Andy.

'Have I? I was saying that the fuss of the crowds in sports stadiums distresses me, it seems so pathetic. They make a great hero of a boxer. They watch one man striking, punching another with gloved fists like smooth knives. One is the champion-priest, the other the victim. It distresses me.'

I, the Beggar, inserted words akin to what he had said into the depths of his consciousness and he listened. It was a habitual way of communicating across an abyss of fact and fiction but few paid any attention to what was happening in them.

'They are totally oblivious' – *he continued translating what I was telling him* – 'of the music their voices create across distances when they roar their wild applause; a music like rain and fire in rapids. Do you follow, Andy?'

My silent speech had touched George's subconscious mind. Had he not translated my dark words – in some degree – into speech? But he was uneasy, very uneasy. *So was I.* We were sketching in elements of Nature of which we knew little. What are the elements of Nature? How various are they? Andy was deeply puzzled and yet he too had been unable to avoid a slight but real commotion arising in a work of Art that I embodied. George, Andy knew, was an impractical person. He had been speaking from outside himself as if a cloud from another country of the Mind had descended and lay upon his words. He seemed to have imbibed the unconscious in the painting. There was no accounting for it. All this could lead far and deep into an adventure which could prove unsettling and which Christopher felt must be stopped at all costs. Andy wondered which way he should go . . .

He remembered that George had insisted there were different *gravities of the Mind*. There was mind – subconscious mind – which was but a trace of Mind, the darkness of Mind possessing unconscious links with the Sun and the Brain. If those links could be adequately explored would they not bring a different world into play? A nonsensical idea, Andy felt, but it made him curiously excited, possibly unhappy nevertheless.

George was something of a wanderer in a minimal sort of way. *He shared a kinship with the Wanderer I was soon to meet as I, the Beggar, shared vestiges of profound creativity with the Artist who had painted me into his canvas.*

George had said to Andy that if one visited another planet one could not survive unless one wore different clothing, wholly different clothing, to help one withstand the gravity there that differed from the Earth's pull on one's feet. There were other things one would have to do that were written into the celestial unconscious . . . But in terms of gravity, George said, there was a parallel with peoples on Earth and in Cities. Not literally, of course, but in shades and values. Perhaps one needed an immaterial clothing – sprung from a new work of Art – involving threads and resemblances in all ruined and active masks one wore to bring peoples together in the creation of a New World.

A nonsensical idea, Andy felt, but it made him greatly uneasy. 'You're becoming obsessed, George,' Andy said at last. 'I wonder what Christopher would say if he were here today. He would be furious. May I say I do understand how you feel revolted by a boxing match and the crowds that go. But you're taking all this too far . . .'

George looked pensive. He was staring into the canvas and listening inwardly. Something seemed to speak. Was it beside him? Was it in the canvas? Whatever it was he felt it was incomplete. Where would such incompletion lead?

'Tell them', I whispered, 'it's an obscure, incomplete religion as far as the crowds are concerned but if you said so to them, you would be treated like a lunatic, George. We all suffer from incomplete religions – some claim to be absolute and are in the open and do not have to hide in sports stadiums. I wish I understood better. I wish I could tell you more . . .'

George was staring at my rags that were blown like thick clouds, he felt, in the commotion of the canvas. He remembered the South American skies that seemed to bring a red message of sunrise (despite sunset). The skies were torn with the memory of agonising beauty staining trees and waters. No wonder there were pyramids of the Sun in Mexico and Peru.

The pyramids were deserted now by priests and victims but bands, claiming to be Incas, could be seen with swastikas on their sleeves. Were they totalitarian rebels defying totalitarian rulers? The pathos of a desolated humanity! Were they shadows protesting against the shadows of the past? Were they political/religious entertainers at the edge of two worlds, one visible, the other invisible?

'An obscure religious faith!' George said to himself inwardly. 'Could this be true of the bands I saw in Peru and the crowds in sports stadiums in the City? I cannot believe it. What is religious faith? Is it something in Nature that affects us so compulsively, so blindly, we need an Art to unravel its complex proportions? If I were to tell Andy how I now feel, he would laugh his head off. And rightly so perhaps. Who would believe that the crowds in great sports stadiums are involved in a religious ritual of which they are ignorant? No, I must not be hasty. I must give myself time to think.'

'*Time to think,*' I agreed. '*But thinking is opening your mind to possibilities you never dreamt existed in you and beyond you. We shall help each other to bring together parts of our natures that are incomplete.*' It was a curious confession for me, a Beggar in a painting, to make. What is Art that does not learn from those who are involved in reading it, in studying it?

I continued speaking silently as in a dream – '*We are uneasy about obscure religious customs in sport. Let us go to a centre where a boxer is in training for a fight. See how curiously reverent everyone is. They watch the boxer putting on his gloves and one cannot tell what they really see. What do we see?*'

George listened. He looked around, in his dream, and saw a man with smooth gloves punching away at a stuffed balloon hanging from the ceiling. He awoke, it seemed, and turned to Andy.

'Do we sleep in broad daylight?' he asked. 'Sleep or dream? Perhaps I am obsessed, Andy. A stuffed balloon! It differs from the image in this painting and yet it carries a hidden – not so hidden – resemblance . . .'

'What are you getting at?'

'I dreamt I saw a man punching/striking a headless, limbless body – a stuffed balloon if you like – that was hanging from the ceiling!'

'There's nothing that isn't quite ordinary in what you say,' said Andy in a mist of practicality. 'That's how boxers train. They have to focus on specific points in a body that they fight.'

'It's funny,' said George, 'when you look into the painting as into a dream. It's funny to see the headless, limbless body in a stuffed balloon . . . Isn't it the caricature of a goddess?'

George said no more but Andy was astonished. He too was staring into the canvas at the ancient, violin-shaped figure he saw there but it apparently meant nothing to him. Did it mean

64

anything to him? The mist of practicality in which he moved had erased all vestiges of a resemblance, essential and therefore hidden, superficial and therefore plain. 'I shall ask Christopher when he comes tomorrow what he makes of this.'

George was stirred to reply: 'It's an ancient religious custom they have changed from prayer to violence. No one remembers save in a work of Art . . .'

'Remembers what? Headlessness, limblessness? Damned cruel, if you ask me!'

'Not cruelty,' said George. 'Pathos! The pathos of humanity.' *He spoke in himself now after listening to my silent words in the painting, coming from beside him it seemed.* 'Does anyone know where he or she has come from in universal, immaterial/material senses? Better a boxing ring and a balloon today than to be burnt at the stake yesterday.'

5

There came the sound of a great mass of people approaching the gallery in the street below us. George and Andy moved to the window. I followed and placed myself between them. It was a trick I played in placing myself as Nothing whereas I knew I was Something. I was a Nobody with a voice which touched George in particular. I was invisible as all Nobodies should be except in a painting or in the theatre where I could be rendered exactly in the garment or cloth I appeared to wear.

I asked questions of myself through George.

Who was I? How could I account for myself? I had asked myself these questions before but there are no stopping points to the nature of Art.

Am I an actor in the *Art of the City?* Do I come in the evenings when Christopher, George and Andy are not there? Christopher swears he will bring the play to a stop before it gets into public view in the theatre.

I am invisible to George and Andy, visible to Christopher Columbus. Visibility/invisibility seems irreconcilable but does this not affirm an incomplete theatre one sees and hears which distinguishes my existence? Christopher has seen me in the dress of the Trickster and the Beggar and has heard me speak. George, and possibly Andy, have heard my voice within themselves like a radio of the mind, the subconscious/unconscious mind of theatre.

Speech and dress are two aspects of the incomplete life of the theatre.

Who or what is George? George is a minimal wanderer who will come into larger play in the Wanderer. They are both incomplete. The Trickster is incomplete. Tiresias is incomplete. The Beggar is incomplete. (Am I the Trickster and the Beggar?) Their and my counter-intuitive players may be hidden in the *Art of the City* – and in *History* – but they are there nevertheless.

I am the ghost of memory and I search for the Nature of natures to salvage the wreck of a ship . . . Memory is the trail of incompletion in which I live – and others live through me – in dream and action.

We waited – three of us where stood two – and soon there appeared a million faces in the street. Was this an exaggeration – a million faces – or was it a sign that Art had subtly and ironically extended itself from the canvas on the wall and taken over my estimate of numbers? Three become two and a thousand become a million!

Then we perceived a skeleton ship – borne on shoulders protruding from the crowd – on which had been put the effigy of a boxer staring up at me with pale eyes.

'Good Lord,' said Andy, 'Jason is dead.'

George was utterly astonished. I felt the painting on the wall had pulled the street into the canvas like a thread on which small men and women moved in vast numbers. They (George and Andy) perceived the City as local and factual, I – on the other hand – perceived it as ancient as a stroke of paint which combines everything in a moment, combines the crowds that took Christ to the Cross, combines the crowds that swarmed into the Coliseum in Rome.

'Don't you see the banners they are carrying?' Andy exclaimed. 'The champion was dealt a grievous blow. Like a heavy timber from a rotting ship . . .'

Was the boxer a hero? I had scoffed at this before when I spoke to George (or was it George who spoke to me?) of the pathos of humanity but now it assumed a different and terrible light. Dying had promoted the boxer onto new scales of death and life.

What is the ship? Is it Jason's ship after he gains the Golden Fleece and is stricken by Medea? *The ship is a slave-ship in which slaves travel across the seas in a death that proves to be a terrifying bondage called life.* The slaves are engineered by this death-in-life to fight in sports stadiums when they are 'free'. Their fists are sharp as the knives of a priest and hard as timber in a sacred ship echoing distant histories of which they know nothing. The hidden times, however, fill their blood with unconscious relevance to ancient Greece, to ancient America, to ancient Africa. They are black heroes in a world that has forgotten innate heroism and immaterial love.

'*Are they bringing the effigy to the gallery?' I whispered to George. 'It's a rude piece at the moment but perhaps they anticipate a fine sculpture later on.*' It was a wicked, silent remark tinged with the remembrance of violence and waste.

George did not hear me, it seemed, though what I said got through into his subconscious. Other voices in the street were ringing in his ears.

We were all, I felt, in a painting of history – though few of us, if any, realised it – a painting with positions in which the factual and the local became immeasurable.

Immeasurable! Did the immeasurable signify a 'dumbness' in words as they stumble into the mystery of Art? Nothing was real for me yet everything was real. Had I not stared for ages from the painting into the City? I had never been met before by an answering stare, pale-eyed or otherwise, from a champion who had been felled in a stadium. That blow alone – like a mortal/immortal wound on a battleship or a battlefield – converted me into seeing him as a hero. It was peculiar, it was pathetic, but there it was. That's how he gained an eye to stare back at me from the City, from a monument or an effigy. It may have seemed a small event – a fighter dying in the ring in which he was engineered to fight and bringing immature peoples into mourning – but it loomed far beyond such factuality in a work of Art skewered for the ironic and the universal.

I listened to what George and Andy were saying as though I stumbled into speech myself within myself. Were not words 'dumb' in the 'immeasurable'? How could one speak in a mystery of broken-ness within which all proportions become self-critical and immeasurable in range and context within/beyond the limits of one or the other self? Profoundest creativity was needed.

George had been speaking all along and now he was asking Andy – 'Are they bringing the effigy into the gallery? Perhaps they will make a great head . . .'

'Don't be ridiculous, George. Where do you get such outrageous ideas from? This is a respectable gallery.'

'I saw the ship and I wondered. How was the Olmec head transported?'

'Don't worry about the Olmec head, George. Let me tell you this: the ship means nothing. Ships cannot sail on dry land. Crowds take over. Someone suggested a ship out of the blue, I would imagine. The people were flabbergasted by what had happened to the champion. They took it without thinking. Something in their blood perhaps, who knows? You know anything can happen when you have a big crowd. People are swept along as if by magic. But it will pass soon and they will see how silly they have been.'

'I have to confess,' said George slowly, 'I am more drawn to black Jason now that he has died than when he was fighting in the ring. It's as if' – he hesitated – 'he seems to have put off his dress . . .'

'What do you mean by "dress"?'

'What do I mean by "dress"? A very difficult question to answer. By "dress" I am saying he's no longer cluttered up . . .' He stopped. He felt the dumbness of Art in his mouth. Andy said: 'You're talking in ragged sentences, George. You're mixing everything up.' He smiled and made what seemed a joke. 'The Beggar in the canvas is speaking through you, George.'

'Now that he has died a number of things come into view. I see him as . . .' He stopped again.

'See him as?' Andy probed. 'See him as what?'

'I see him as something he never knew when he was champion. Now that the props of heroism have fallen away he speaks nothing but the naked truth. Forgive me, I do not understand what I am saying.'

I whispered silently in him, with him – 'He's like an unselfconscious, naked Arawak who has no dress, who does not wear the dress of the priest nor of the victim. Columbus saw but did not see what such unselfconsciousness mirrors though it is tinged with scars and terrible memories.'

'Jason is free,' George said, looking deep into the canvas on the wall. He was suddenly startled by what he saw in the painting. He had known of it all along but had not calculated on its range into apparently alien cultures and forms. He turned to Andy – 'By the Almighty,' he said with a cry in his voice, 'I have been blind. I see and I do not see . . .'

'What do you see?'

'I see the man – he's now dressed as the Beggar in rags – who was shot as a terrorist and who falls into the painting on the edges of death and life and who lives. I see him in a new way.'

'Christopher says the Beggar he met in this room has learnt nothing from the painting but gross heresy.'

'Christopher knows and does not want to know. Don't you see, Andy, that the champion – who dies in the ring – falls into an effigy and lives for an instant – which passes quickly I know – but which tells us much of the psyche of the ordinary people? Pathetic they may be but they have an inner, deep, irrational compulsion towards creativity that I, for one, have overlooked. They *see* (without knowing what they see) the instant imprint which passes quickly, as I said, and they seek, without knowing why they seek, to create a sculpture or a monument in a crude effigy. The two things are inseparable. The great painting on the wall and the effigy on a skeleton ship! Not only that! Do you know anything of Michelangelo's last Pietà? It's called the *Rondanini Pietà*. He was eighty-nine when he sculpted this. Christ seems faintly alive, he supports his mother who seems to have died. All this proves, in my estimation, that we do not know the broken-ness in the living and the dying . . .'

'Come, come, George, you're terribly excited. Are you sure that Michelangelo meant his last Pietà to be seen in the way you describe?'

'My dear Andy,' said George, 'the sculpture speaks for itself. It is in league, in some degree, with the Byzantine holiest icon in which a reversal occurs in the Western imagery of the Pietà. Christ, the dying son – in the Byzantine icon – gives re-birth to his dying mother, who has become a Child.'

Andy was puzzled and sceptical. 'What do you make of all this, George?' he asked. 'The Beggar in the painting seems ready to step out and to stand beside you. *Is he real?*'

George hesitated. Then he looked at Andy and replied: 'I said I saw the Beggar in a new way. I mean the man who was shot and who fell into the painting. By "new way" I mean he cannot be captured or seized. That's a part of what I mean. He has to be reinterpreted every century, every generation. His *essence* is beyond us. That's what the painting is saying. One may see, rarely perhaps, an *imprint* that compels us to create, to reinterpret. That *imprint* is available to all, to the great and to the ordinary (if I may put it like that). I have re-interpreted the Byzantine icon. Others may see it differently. The *imprint* shifts from mother to son and back again. As it does with the Beggar. It shifts to Tiresias, to the Trickster, it shifts everywhere. They are all incomplete . . . You ask me if the Beggar is real. *Yes, he is. Real and unreal . . .*'

'Ah!' said Andy. 'What does *real* and *unreal* imply? I am puzzled.'

'It implies', said George, 'an open door to the mystery of truth. Truth is an Art we scarcely understand.'

'Are you telling me that *reality and unreality* are an open door? Quite extraordinary!'

'Yes, I am. There are no absolutes.'

71

'Ah! that's why Christopher would destroy the play . . .'

'There are no absolutes,' George insisted. *'Reality and unreality* imply an endless journey into the mystery of truth.' He stopped. He was searching for further ideas to demonstrate how he felt. 'Think of the sacred ship.'

Andy interrupted – 'What sacred ship? It's a *skeleton* vessel that the crowd brings. A rotting vessel – so it seemed to me.'

'It carries open doors', George cried, 'into seas where Cities are hid, into unknown spaces, into unknown places. It is a skeleton, as you say, it is ruined by wars, by slaveries, so to speak, by misadventures sprung from human blindness. Does this not suggest a creativity beyond devices that halt the mind of the crew? We can repair the ship but we may not see where it is taking us from Old Worlds into New . . .'

George felt a strange, inner excitement. He sensed delicate powers in himself that made him a wanderer, an incomplete version of the Wanderer *I, the Beggar, would soon meet. Was not the Wanderer himself incomplete . . .? I would know soon enough.*

Andy's discomfiture was plain however much he sought to hide it. George was aware of this and he called to him: 'You feel I am fantasising the fighter in the ring, do you not, Andy? I see your point of view. Perhaps you know how Jason became a boxer . . .'

Andy smiled. The mist of practicality which he cultivated was settling on him again. 'Jason has become a fantasy figure for you, George, yes. Is he not a real man?' He spoke quizzically, if not provocatively. 'What I know of Jason's early career in boxing I have learnt from Christopher.'

George was surprised. Andy continued quickly: 'Christopher met him in a café in the City. Jason's wife was there. A brown-skinned woman in a low-cut dress that revealed her breasts. Christopher felt she was a prostitute. A kind of witch!' He gave a slight, sceptical laugh. 'Christopher is a religious fanatic, as you know. However, he went on to tell me that she had promised to help her husband become a champion.'

George was even more surprised. 'An odd business,' he said. 'What help would she give him?'

'I do not know,' Andy confessed, 'but she gave the word of a witch' – he laughed again, this time more openly – 'that he would achieve championship and could hold it, until he retired, if he remained constant and faithful to her.'

'You laugh,' said George, 'but I find it odd. He has become a champion . . .'

'They met many years ago,' Andy continued. 'Jason was no more than eighteen then. This year he is thirty-two or thirty-three. They met at a table in the café. His wife was there, as I said before. She listened as Jason spoke but said not a word. Christopher much disliked her. He said she would abuse herself.'

'Abuse herself!' George exclaimed.

Andy sought to defend, in some degree, Christopher's outlandish statement – 'A witch treads on burning coals, does she not? Is this not a threat of abuse?' The edge of laughter shook his lips. 'Anyway, as you know, Jason did become the champion and was loved by the crowds which attended his fights. Whether this has anything to do with his wife, the witch – as Christopher called her – is another question. He took up with another woman – that is true – and neglected his wife. I remember Christopher telling me – some time later – that they quarrelled bitterly in the street below where the crowds now pass. I remember this because he spoke of the Beggar who arrived suddenly in the gallery when the scene in the street was at its worst. Jason stopped, when the Beggar arrived, and went away and left his wife close to the monument in the park below.' He was laughing again. 'You would think it was all part of a play! Perhaps the Beggar rescued her. Who can say?' He laughed again. 'Rescued her without altogether knowing that he did so.'

'Indeed, he was dressed exactly as in the painting! He had come to study the canvas for the part he played in the rehearsals at night when we and Christopher were away.

They had a fierce row in the gallery and this convinced Christopher more than ever that the play must not be seen by the public.'

'Did Christopher have anything more to say?'

Andy seemed to hesitate before replying. Then he said, 'No, nothing more, though he appeared to be on the verge of telling me something but he desisted.'

I, the Beggar, who had been standing invisible between them now moved away from them. Had I rescued Jason's wife without altogether knowing that I did so? Would she appear in another light – that would astonish me – within or beneath the Darkness of the world? George was conscious of a vacancy as I left them alone. A vacancy? Where is that vacancy? In that 'vacancy' hopped 'one' and 'we'. In that 'hop' George felt himself to be 'one' or 'we': an instinctive eccentricity in 'incompletions' (which he kept to himself) reaching back across ages in the manifold play of the Arts.

Thus it is that 'one' (or 'we') may be left 'vacant' without quite knowing when or where. The art of dying is an art of 'vacancy'. 'One' dies a little every day. Such 'dying' implies a 'presence' one cannot see which moves away and leaves an 'emptiness'.

Death then is wholly real for the 'individual' body which sees itself as perfectly whole. But it may not be for the 'incomplete' self which still stands before the painting on the wall and feels something is missing in its gaze and attention: something that had addressed the ear of the mind perhaps but has now departed, something in another self . . .

Such a 'gaze', such 'attention', seem curiously invalid until the 'ear' realises they and itself are vital parts of a play to be reinterpreted across ages in 'vacancies' that loom suddenly and leave us hollow and 'empty'. We slide into individual death even as the incomplete self inherits emptiness as a new opening for presence, for another re-shaping of a broken self . . .

What is 'presence'?

'Presence' is an unconscious, small manifestation of a gigantic play in which – whether we know it or not – we live and die and are imprinted by immortal Art.

, Our *essence* cannot be stolen or captured. It leans on 'vacancies' as a measure of the reinterpretation of form, of substance, beyond the million and more individual bodies which perish every year.

'Incompletion' reaches from the visible to the invisible, the real to the unreal, speech to silence, and has no absolute boundaries. It re-shapes itself into new roles it plays that carry but a hint of the universal play from which it comes.

All this gives a hint of our ceaseless struggle to understand ourselves, of George's deep unease with Andy's quizzical and sceptical reports of Jason and his wife. Yet even Andy had spoken – without quite knowing what he was saying – of an ancient play he vaguely felt could be linked, in Jason's death, to the painting on the wall.

One's mind was prickled by the question: what was it that Christopher Columbus concealed in his unsatisfactory report to the world of the strangers he had met in the land of the Arawaks?

Those strangers became – in Andy's address to George – modern citizens in a City in which Jason, the boxer, was killed by Medea. He had fallen in the ring at the hand of another boxer but his end lay in the fateful outcome brought into play by the betrayal of his wife. George felt this but he could say nothing of it to Andy. He did not have the words, he did not know how to put it, to make it truer than any rational dis-course that operated in the mists of Andy's brain and sun of practicality.

I, the Beggar, felt I could raise this with the Wanderer whom I would soon meet.

We – the Arawaks and I – came upon him at last sitting at a door to Olmec City. The River ran past painted smooth as a pavement. He waved the Arawaks through the door but kept me outside. 'You shall see them later,' he said.

He had rather bushy, smouldering hair on his cheeks. His skin was burnt by the sun. He was dressed in a green garment that was burning at the edges with painted effect. His eyes appeared also to be green as they glanced at me. Had they been painted or were they a reflection of the fire of psyche I glimpsed in his wanderings? He may have been forty or fifty. It was difficult to tell. We were both characters painted in the canvas but I had not seen him before. This was something with which I was familiar. Many areas of the painting seemed to be new as though they had been placed there recently. It was an old (possibly ancient) canvas. Who could have added what seemed new? Were my eyes blind to visionary developments that were there in the beginning but never understood or creatively seen? One sees and still does not see. One reads and still does not read. I had asked these questions before but there was no answer. Would the Wanderer give me a clue or an answer? I felt I must listen closely to what he said.

'Tiresias told me that we would meet but he left before I could question him further. He spoke of the Lovers. Where are they? I am not sure of everything he said. Is that not the way of things? Everyone makes errors in a search for the truth. Perhaps there are no Lovers. Perhaps it was a dream. One may be wonderfully inspired – as Tiresias is – but what one says is never absolute. All bibles carry the words of inspired men who inevitably made grievous errors in their poetry and prophecy. I am glad we have met. You travel everywhere, do you not? It is fortunate you are here at this time. Forgive me – what do I mean by *at this time*? Time is a bubble or a series of bubbles. Some seem replete with happiness, others are filled with sorrow. I am glad you are here like a miracle of presence in a vortex of times . . .' I stopped. I could say no more.

The Wanderer was looking at me closely. 'You are the ghost of memory, are you not? You were shot as a terrorist and you fell into the painting. That was new. This is an old canvas. Have you been here in the beginning unseen, hidden by arrows, spears, guns, bullets? You ask about the Lovers! But first you must ask: *What is Love?* Unless you can truly say what love is, there are no Lovers!'

'Who are you?' I cried.

'I am the ghost of fire. I may have fallen myself into the painting – fallen in flames and ignored as an outrage. Now that I am a little clearer, within the vortex of air and fire, you have met me. Such is the mystery of Art. How did you become a terrorist? You are *not* a terrorist!' He looked deep into me and into worlds on which I stood. 'You are mixed up in wars that are occurring (or have been happening for ages) between hostile armies in which *hate* drives men to do things they would not otherwise do. All worlds at war – secretly or openly – are burning at their edges and within. Do I not – in the mysterious emerging of Man from flames – make this somewhat clearer?'

'I see you now – for the first time – in this painting of histories . . .' I said, emphasising as best I could what he had been saying.

'Yes, I know. You shall see more in a light when the Darkness blazes . . .'

'What do you mean?'

'We live in a dangerous bubble of time. The green world is in great danger. Consciousness and the unconscious re-shape themselves endlessly into a play or plays, into a myth or myths. Man is a peculiar myth in the re-shaping of himself, I am a myth, you are a myth. Can we read what myths are saying? Can we read *through* every outrage?' The Wanderer brushed the smouldering points of beard off his face. 'It has taken you measureless concentration to see me.' He stopped then continued speaking softly: 'What is fire? Fire is a pro-found element of the gods. Can you see now – after long ages of blindness – why Prometheus was punished? No one saw – and still does not see – within the fires he brought from heaven even a flickering message of hope and remorse from a Mind in Darkness.'

77

He stopped again and I listened closely as he continued –
'Is it the Mind of God? Is there a strange Darkness in the
Mind of God? I speak of gods but am tempted now – for an
instant perhaps – to speak of God! It's an old Promethean play
or myth that may be seen in several ways – the way of the
gods, the way of God encompassing all gods, all bubbles of
time, all extremes to teach us to take nothing for granted and
to give range and depth to human limitations.' He hesitated –
'Is it not true', he said, 'that without the gods, in the absence
of the gods that are partial, God would become so dominant,
so central, he would turn absolutely human and limited?

'Perhaps God blazes a little through the partialities of the
gods to bring home our broken-ness, the deceptions we prac-
tise, the revelations we stumble upon.' He stopped and looked
at me with his green, fiery eyes that resembled the glance of
a Tiger.

'Think!' he said. 'Is Prometheus passive? He is punished by
a god for his passivity. He is still counselled to look *through*
the fires he brings from heaven but he remains blind to what
lies within them. Is he active? He is punished by another god
for the violence in which his lower organs function: cured one
day, extinct the next, extinction/cure, cure/extinction, a perpetual and cruel oscillation of the fires he brings from heaven.
He glimpses at last a saving resolution and with the help of
still another god is able to change into a rock, or a monument,
or a head, in Olmec City. This wholly new development (is it
new? is it old?) foreshadows a far-reaching possibility for a
goddess who walks on water in the painting on the walls of
the gallery.'

6

The Wanderer opened the door of the room in Olmec City into which he had sent the Arawaks.

Does the light in a Dream (which is logically dark since one's eyes are closed) become so real that the characters speak as if they are outside the Dream though they are within? So does the light that baffles one's eyes in a painting create excessive within-ness/without-ness to which the Wanderer and I now belong. We speak with tongues of dark light, we see with eyes of painted light. Is this not a version of the myth of Mankind living, re-living itself in Dream and levels of dark sight within the room of history?

The room into which I was looking was very dark. My inner eyes soon grew accustomed to the darkness and I perceived vagaries of light everywhere. The light seemed to flicker (as if it had arisen from a fire in a head of stone) and to settle into shapes beyond its freakish behaviour. The Arawaks materialised into apparently firm bodies.

'They look stronger,' I said, 'fresher, more vigorous. Not that they were not strong before but something has happened that gives them new impetus. It's amazing when I consider the vagaries of paint from which they emerge. Are my eyes – inner/outer – changing to allow me to see (with consciousness and unconsciousness) new things in an old canvas? This is a question I have asked myself before but I am so astonished now I find I must ask it again.'

The Wanderer pointed into the middle of the room. 'It's Elena/Medea,' he said. 'You look at her and you know of a broken-ness in your normal eyesight. It's odd, isn't it? You *know* now of that broken-ness. It becomes – how shall I put it? – a glass. Yes, let's say a glass! You find yourself looking *through* that glass at a miracle of possibilities! Have you sensed this earlier? Perhaps you have but you have not reflected fully on passages of mysterious light that seem to tie you in yet release you in the City. Release others as well. They seem to belong to distances you have never really considered. The Arawaks suddenly look stronger. You begin – unconsciously perhaps (the unconscious rising like a tide into consciousness) – to review the past and to see creatures (human and others) as they may have been before they disappeared under the blind weight of the Conquistadores. It's a vision on one side of your-self into a dimension which seems utterly closed on the other side, yet it opens slowly as this door does . . .'

I listened – as in a Dream – to what the Wanderer was saying. 'Do you mean', I said, 'that Elena/Medea is such a marvellous painter of doors opening into a room?' I peered into the middle of the room into which the Wanderer was pointing.

'She is *more* than a painter,' he replied. 'She has gone *beyond* the Artist's intentions.' He stopped and appeared to reflect on what he had said.

'But how could this be?' I asked. 'It sounds impossible.'

'Are quantum realities impossible? You are a quantum myth. I am as well.' He stopped and looked at me as I looked into the room. 'I am simply saying that the Artist *knows* he has come to the end of a visionary path and this inner knowl-edge equips him to attune himself to people and things he has painted which turn on him now and bring new visionary pos-sibilities into his fingers, into the brush with which he paints, into the eyes with which he sees, as though he becomes a new creator and is re-created by what he assumes are his creations. Elena/Medea is much more than he first intended . . .'

I interrupted and said somewhat haltingly, 'Are you telling me' – I paused a little – 'Are you telling me' – I paused again – 'that the Artist is peculiarly limited' – I stopped once again – 'that his genius lies in a profound awareness of his limitations affecting ends and beginnings which he *partially* creates and which turn on him and lead him in another direction? I wish I could put it exactly but then . . .' I stopped. I was peering into the middle of the miraculous room. The vagaries of light were still there – or had started afresh – but had settled upon the Promethean rock or head upon which stood the flickering, excessive sculpture of a woman.

'Do you see her?' asked the Wanderer.

'Yes, I do,' I said but with acute uncertainty. 'Is she standing on an Olmec head? This seems to have changed somewhat. It has a blade of fire and a blade of water mingling in the glass of my eyes. It's the same Olmec head and yet quite different.'

'She is alive,' the Wanderer exclaimed. '*She is alive*. She stands on a transformed rock – as you now see it – in a sea of light. The fires Prometheus brought from heaven light the seas into an oceanic stairway on which she treads and rises. Elena/Medea walks on this shifting ladder as she has never done before or – if she has – no one saw her do it in past ages.'

'She looks like a sculpture,' I said, peering into the room.

'Do you not see', cried the Wanderer, 'how she moves? Do you not see how her feet move?'

I stared into the room and considered the woman on the rock which had been fired into a stairway or a ladder. I was painted myself, I knew, on the waving edges of a broken life. I had travelled on this precarious stairway on which men and women knew me, as related to themselves, or did not know me in an eclipse of an area in themselves. The sculpture of the woman – as it seemed to me in the trembling light – was a combination of flesh and of shuddering water.

Why had I not seen it? Had I too lost a subtle part of myself with others in the eclipse of our journey from sea to land? Had we accumulated biases of ignorance which made it difficult, if not impossible, to judge our steps on the ladder of the sea?

We had come from the sea – we had belongings in the sea – but this was purely a technical matter that did not touch us inwardly except in a profound, new/old work of Art.

I glimpsed now (or thought I glimpsed) – despite losses of the shaking ladder of the sea – a goddess of incredible poise and grace. She was moving gently on the sea of light, upon the lights of water, resembling stars and distant suns, glittering, rising, falling. The lines of her body shifted in the sea.

'I know of Medea,' I cried, thinking of Jason, the boxer, and of his wife who had slain him. 'But who is Elena?'

'Elena is Venezuelan. Her name brings further relevance to Medea's possibilities history has underestimated. Elena/Medea walks on water. The wave of an infinite ocean is in her blood.'

'Is she a witch?' I cried. I felt I must defy what I had seen (or thought I had seen). 'Is she a prostitute and a witch? Does she kill those she deeply dislikes?' I knew I had put the question unjustly, capriciously. I had forgotten much. The Wanderer was startled. He weighed the term 'witch' in his mind.

'Ah! I see,' he said at last. 'Jesus walked on water but he was not regarded as a witch or a wizard. If a woman had done so, at that time, when women were stoned for sleeping with men to whom they were not married, she would have been seen as a witch.'

'Was Medea a witch?' I demanded with a sense of outrage at my own ignorance. I was stiflingly aghast (as though I had caught a cold) by a prejudice, a bias in myself which made me blind to what I had seen and done in the past.

The Wanderer became grave. 'What is a witch?' He was silent. 'What is a witch?' he repeated. 'If a woman had walked on water – as I said a short while ago – in the age of Christ, she would have been deemed a witch. *You* have had the sensation of walking on air, have you not? I know it was only a dream-sensation! Is not life itself a dream we do not understand? Are there not mysteries in Nature? How can I explain to you what your inner pulse has known, what your inner eyes have seen?'

I was filled with remorse. 'Forgive me!' I said. 'You are quite right! How shall I put it?' I felt the speaking light on my tongue disappearing. But it glowed again in my mouth as if painted afresh by the brush of Nature. 'I *have* seen the woman walk on water. But I am still uncertain, still unsure, of what I have seen. There is a Darkness which blazes but a little in the room and this gives me an imperfect sense of things. Are my inner eyes permanently broken? Does this painting into which I have fallen express the fallacies – that border on the glory – of Mankind? *Is glory an illusion?* The Darkness in the room – the Darkness of Mind in the world – affects . . .' I stopped again.

'I must confess,' I said, 'the woman is – how shall I put it? – beautiful. But with a beauty that disengages our ideas of fixed beauty. Her beauty goes beyond sexual charm or manners. Am I really conscious of her poise, her grace? How could she have such poise when the shaking ladder in the lighted waves in the room defies all men who would have her, who would *eat* her, if they could, as a choice article of meat?' I stopped. What had I been saying? I was confused.

The Wanderer was silent. He deeply understood my confusion in the light, in the Darkness, in the new-found Promethean fires, which gave the painting both a curious relevance and a curious ambiguity to inner vision and to inner understanding in regard to the breaching of fixed values associated with ancient/modern histories.

He looked at me across the canvas with his green, burning eyes as if he were addressing a world beyond me but within me.

'There is something you may have forgotten,' he said, 'but which you may now be able to face. Who am I? Am I in the painting, as all artists are, when they paint the old and the new? What I have to tell you is here in the painting, but who sees it? You have not seen it before. Medea is a goddess . . . How do you understand this when she has killed Jason's and her two children? The gods – despite their diversity – saw through her and took her to heaven. They honoured her. Why did they?'

I did not reply immediately but I became aware of the craft in the Wanderer's elusive body and mind. I studied afresh his green dress, his smouldering beard. I studied the slightly burning edges of the garment he wore. I was not only aware of his craft but bowled over inwardly as I had been in the rapids. He seemed to know the Trickster, he seemed to know Tiresias, he seemed to know me. He seemed to know us all in ways that were astonishing. *Was he the Artist?* Did his ghost dwell in the painting? Did he embody the mystery of a creator and his creation in which consciousness and unconsciousness were not contrivances but essential, uncapturable forces playing tricks upon us which we assumed were normalities? Was he present in the work he may have created even though he was absent? He was a quantum Artist . . .

Was his presence a trick of consciousness and his absence a trick of paint that gave him unconscious reality? Did the reality of the unconscious turn on consciousness in fire and water of devastating proportions even as we sought to contain them in symbols and signs that we adopted in religious and cultural rituals? In what degree were we deceiving ourselves about the Nature of truth which required a ceaseless probe into consciousness and unconsciousness beyond and within ourselves?

I had probed 'presence' before but now the Wanderer touched upon apparently undreamt-of and immensely important perspectives. He had drawn me through a crafted labyrinth, he had exercised subtle controls over me, he had drawn me to peer into the most extraordinary room in Olmec City, and yet I knew – as a quantum creature in a quantum creation – that I possessed a peculiar independence and was capable of turning on him and making him paint differently as if I myself were involved in the arts of creation – involved in an involuntary force of the unconscious beyond myself and within myself.

These were staggering truths (beyond the logic of material reason) which helped me to see *into* plays, *into* myths, that

84

were taken as *outer* performances whereas they were disguises by which men fooled themselves about the turning unconscious on the conscious.

The Wanderer had brought Promethean fires into a shaking and slightly blazing Darkness of the Mind of God (resembling laddered lights in a sea). In such lights I had known illusions of glory, I had seen but not comprehended fully what I had seen. Now, however, I felt a new but uneasy confidence working within myself. I could speak with real/unreal authority, as a creature of myth, of the room I had seen. I could speak to Christopher Columbus like an eruption of the unconscious in him pleading with him and against which he fought. Would he change at the last moment, would we change, and release a true phantom of saving Art, a true phantom of forces beyond capture in a world we shared?

'This door you have opened into a room', I said at last to the Wanderer, 'is the most crucial opening in the painting. It brings illusion and truth that intertwine with each other, it brings deceptions leading to realities, so much so that Art speaks through us – through our appearances as painted flesh or fleshy paint – of the immense journey of life.'

'Does it?' said the Wanderer.

'Is there not a deception in the room pointing to a remarkable inner truth? The gods deceive to reveal. Truth is stranger than hard-and-fast reason.'

'Is it?' said the Wanderer.

'Is the Arawak woman in the room – whom you call Elena/Medea – an ancient and a modern fabrication of subtle pieces drawn together from many legends? What is her principal legend?'

'You have put your finger', said the Wanderer, 'on a matter that relates closely to the question I asked about Medea whom the gods honoured.

'There are many legends we do not acknowledge fully in her make-up. She was gifted by Nature to help Jason gain the Golden Fleece but he betrayed her. This betrayal leaves her alone. *What is Love?* The Lovers are not realised. Some faiths that have ruled the world cling to a male priest without a wife. She clings to a goddess we must come to know – by degrees of confession in ourselves – without a husband. And in clinging she changes and asks: *What is Love?*

'I have travelled many worlds – not as a tourist – but as a living member of grief-stricken societies in which I found myself. I studied the legend of women bearing strings of babies, one each year, year after year, until they died from exhaustion. Their husbands seemed not to care. *What is Love?*

'I studied the legend of child-labour in farms in poor countries, the legend of children bundled into factories, bundled as they grew into immaturity into navies and armies. *What is Love?*

'I studied the legend of women who wanted to become pregnant to prove to their neighbours they were not infertile, and of men who wanted their wives to conceive so that they might have sons. Such men were kings in their houses. *What is Love?*

'All these legends, and many more, are broken by Medea who confessed to slaying her two children. Thereby she brought to our attention immemorial, apparently timeless frames *to which we do not confess. What is Love?*

'It was a terrible act on her part. But she exposed her inner being and the world's inner being. She broke in herself a fixed trail of habits in which we frame an infant before it is born.

'What is her principal legend? You ask this! I would say it is an *inner, phantom* shattering and differentiation of frames that seem changeless in material, human logic. How then can they change? Perhaps they do not change except at the other extreme – in an extreme goddess – where the witch-like proportions of the goddess are sensed as also changeless in the commerce of rationality which divides Nature into compartments, human and elemental. Such compartments do not meet and are materialised as eternally separate. But an *inner, phantom* leap brings an impossibility/possibility, a meeting, into play.

'That impossibility/possibility takes over. Art is the phantom of truth that turns on material logic. The world may deceive itself that it changes with cultural, religious symbols. But there is no absolute foundation for the change Medea experiences within herself and beyond herself. She does not deceive herself except as the gods do by deceiving men and women to reveal unparalleled possibilities.

'She helps to revise the Arts of the world by bringing into play doors that open which seem forever shut. Do people see? No one knows. Catastrophe piles up slowly, almost invisibly.

'She finds a *lightness* of foot and wing: a miracle of inwardness. She remembers the Cycladic goddess. *There* is a *lightness* of form we did not consider.

'She becomes *light*, *light* in weight, light as a human bird on every ship, light as a goddess who walks on water. She flew across the sea to the Arawak woman to whom she gave her name Elena/Medea. She helped her on a stairway of the sea as a volcano shed its fleece of stars across the ocean and shook the waters terribly.

'Love began to ache inwardly, to seek to overcome slowly piling catastrophe, to find itself in shaking waters, in damaged soils, everywhere.'

There came a roar from the gallery: 'This is heresy! Heresy! Heresy!'

Christopher Columbus was alone in the gallery. George and Andy had left for lunch. Other visitors who had been studying the painting had also made their way out of the great building. Christopher was now alone and free to vent his spleen.

I stepped out of the canvas reluctantly. I did not wish to leave the Wanderer. We were together in the consciousness/unconsciousness that one perceived in the painting. 'We' and 'one' were linked in all men and women though few were aware of this subtle linkage. Christopher was. He saw me, visible in and out of the painting. He resented bitterly this secret and forbidden knowledge that he possessed. He erased it from his mind but it troubled him unconsciously. He accepted me as one of the players in *Art of the City* as the play (based on the painting) was called.

I needed to learn much more from the Wanderer about my eruption into the gallery from Christopher's troubled unconscious. I was a ghost of memory linked to death and life. He saw me as a material being and dressed me in lines he took from the painting on the wall. Do we not re-make the past in this light and settle for material fixtures of person and place? Do we not settle with one side of ourselves? It was with great sadness that I left the Wanderer in my state of incomplete understanding. Yet I knew – in such incompletion – I was open to new possibilities.

Christopher turned – after a while – and saw me close to the door. I approached him. The humour in his eyes had vanished almost entirely.

He studied my dress and exclaimed: 'You are here again! You have come up once again to inspect the painting. This play of yours! I see you are wearing a green dress over the rags of a Beggar. Are you two-in-one?' There was a crinkle of humour, after all, on his lips.

'Yes,' I said. 'I wear a green dress I borrowed from the Wanderer.' I did not tell him I wished to conceal from him my phantom limbs under the Beggar's rags. 'What do you mean by heresy! You are wrong. There is no heresy.'

He nodded as if he agreed but declared: 'I am right. How could you blame Jesus for the failure of Medea to convince those around her that she was not a witch? What does Medea in any case know of love? How can she begin to question the spirit of love?'

I was exasperated. 'Where did I blame Jesus . . .?'

He interrupted: 'You speak as though you are *in* the play. The Wanderer indeed . . . I hear you talking in the play though I am not in the gallery at nights.'

88

I was astonished. 'How do you *hear*?'

'I know what you are saying. You speak with gestures, with the garments that you wear.'

The garments that you wear! This remark of his – the materials one is given to wear – made me conscious all at once *of how I had been mistaken for and shot as a terrorist!* I had lost my passport and had felt a tide of anxiety rise within me when the armed police approached me. I was South American, Venezuelan/Brazilian. I knew I would be sent away from the City. I felt the rapids in my blood, planes, cars, vehicles of all sorts, floods . . . I was ridden by anxieties. I felt a mortal/immortal sea of fevers within me. I saw a goddess walk towards me before the shot was fired. An all-too-human predicament.

I ran and clung to a monument to save myself from drowning in the seas rising within and about me. And then I felt a fist like a bullet in another man's back. I climbed the monument which was the skeleton mast of a ship and entered the window of the gallery in which Christopher Columbus was peering at the Trickster in the canvas on the wall. The figures on the wall were decaying, it seemed, as I fell from the skeleton mast into them. Had I hidden all this to give unsuspected energy to the work of Art on the wall? The mystery of an incomplete self through others in the dead and the living.

I caught myself within the past in a future that was the present and listened afresh to what Christopher was now saying.

'I have studied', he said, 'every line in the painting. It speaks, yes, it speaks.'

'You have not heard rightly,' I said. 'No one is blaming Christ, who was partly trapped in the age in which he lived. It was a man's world – to put it bluntly. It was implied that if a woman like Medea had lived at that time she would have been shot or stoned or deemed a witch if she had . . .' The fusion of the past, the future, and the present was still strong within me. Christopher interrupted. He cried: 'Medea! Medea! Medea! There is a grave heresy. How can you compare Medea to

Christ? I tell you I have followed every line, every curve, every dot, every colour, every move, in this painting. I have followed it day after day, week after week, month after month, year after year. I have followed it like music. *I* know what it is saying. So do *you* and your colleagues who are preparing and rehearsing the play.'

I walked even closer to the canvas and pointed to the door the Wanderer had opened.

'Do you see that door?' I said. 'It is an extraordinary, testing door. Do you see *me* at the door?'

Christopher looked closely. 'Of course I do. Yes I do. I tell you I know every line in the painting. Even the lines that are beginning to fade. But I do not see the test. Are you preparing this test in the play? I cannot see it.'

'Where is the heresy?' I demanded. 'The Darkness within the room blazes a little to test us. Do you see now what is happening? I wish I knew how best to put it. Cruelty is native to us unless we can learn to see *into* the light that blazes with such uncertainty. We rely absolutely on the Brain of the body extended into the Sun. The Sun or Brain rules us and makes us cruel to ourselves and others. We fear the testing Darkness which can bring a wholesome change if we can fuse it with the Sun and see that fusion in a new, creative universe. I have failed too to understand such a universe. What is this universe? How does it test us? It shows us how small we are, how little we see. The rest is Darkness. The Arawak woman in the room, whose name is Elena/Medea, makes me see myself far back and far forward in a grain of truth. She is married to a testing Nature that destroys horrendously, it would seem, and saves miraculously. She is married to a truth we cannot confine in a single apartment or compartment. It is too vast, too complicated.'

'You are joking,' said Christopher. 'How can we move beyond what we know? Truth is God.'

'I am a fool, I grant.' I hesitated for a moment. 'She walks on water,' I said. '*She walks on water*. Is this not a miracle that leaves us hollow, devastated? Without such hollowness, such devastation, that seems horrific, how can we begin to grow *light*, light in weight, and follow her?'

'Impossible,' cried Christopher. 'Only the Son of God has walked on the sea. Indeed he alone knows what love is.'

I said to Christopher: 'Who am I to question what the Son of God is? He may be a profound symbol of love. But as a grain of truth, fallen into damaged soil, and alive in a small way to the opposites in things, I feel we need a woman – who has become *lights*, light in weight and light in uncertain light – to tell us what love is in the infinite wastes of the universe. She must be able to create a miracle in those wastes.' I spoke with profound pathos. Would Christopher yield to my pleas not to see heresies in the painting into which I had fallen like a grain into damaged figures, the Trickster, the Beggar in rags, and others?

'Stop!' he cried. 'This is where your play is dangerous. It presumes too much. Tell me, where is the heaven of which the painting speaks? Where are the gods?'

I considered the questions he had raised. He had spoken with venom and disdain. I felt, as I listened to him, that something was hanging over his mind that could be disastrous.

'Heaven is a medium,' I said at last, 'which we cannot easily dispense with. It has been there from the beginning of times. The world remains trapped in such simplicities. Heaven is 'up there'. We have technical doubts about what 'up there' is. But such technical misgivings cannot easily heal our broken-ness. Science is a series of technicalities. Has it healed us? I would say therefore that heaven is in Nature, a Nature of complex and difficult balances between all things, all peoples, all creatures, lands and waters, balances through which we may *learn* – with an open mind – to break through in small degrees – however minuscule – the involuntary prisons in which we imprison ourselves.'

'Man is made in the image of God,' Christopher cried. 'This is my conviction. We must fight to uphold it. It gives us strength, it gives us resolution. *Man is made in the image of God.*'

'*Fight!*' I said. 'You have to fight to uphold your absolute. Whom do you fight? You fight others who have *their* absolutes. It is a hopeless situation.'

I felt I was losing the battle (why did I see it as a battle?) to overcome Christopher's mind, which seemed to me to be filled with an impending disaster. Would he fight me? I had no absolutes. Would this help him to break through his ghostly fear and hate of others which paradoxically made them strong?

'Let me ask you once again,' I said. 'Do you see the room in the City that the Wanderer brings into view? It is dark, very dark, I know, but it has a light that brings home the sculpture within.'

'*Sculpture!*' Christopher exclaimed. 'Did you not say *a living woman?*'

'Did I? If I did she is alive . . .'

'Is she a piece of sculpture or a living woman?'

'She is both,' I said desperately. 'How do paintings and sculptures live?'

Christopher was laughing at me.

'How do the paintings on the wall live?' I insisted.

'They live', Christopher said, 'because you make a play with them and people act various roles.'

'Precisely,' I said. 'A play brings a group of figures in a painting into a measure of new life which is still unfinished. A play is also a work of Art. This is the mystery of universal Art which acts through new energies from one medium to another. How do we define those energies? They may come from outside a given medium. They may seem vague, uncertain, but they also arrive from unsuspected sources in the violent world in which we live. Art therefore encompasses the excesses which are notorious and which seem to lie outside the good of a good God.' I pointed at the canvas. 'I was shot as a terrorist and I brought new life into the Trickster . . .'

Christopher had stopped laughing. He looked strangely puzzled and disturbed.

'What is Art?' I continued. 'There are energies which come from anywhere and fall into paintings, sculptures, writings, and make them live afresh. All art is in a state of ruin awaiting the moment when energy comes in afresh. We live in a complicated world. The sculpture in the room *lives* because it is energised by indeterminate sources in ancient and in modern myth and history.'

'How do you intend to put all this into your play? Tell me!'

'It is not *my* play,' I said. 'It is *your* play and everyone else's.'

He interrupted. 'How shall you put it in the play? Tell me!'

'We shall put it, in part, through the indeterminate ship to which Elena/Medea moves in the dark, nebulous room which the Wanderer brings into view. It is an incomplete ship. It is Columbus's ship. It is . . .'

'It is *my* ship,' he cried stubbornly. 'It is *not* incomplete. It was wrecked and lies beneath the waves of the sea but I have re-built it completely.'

'You deny your *inner* imagination, Christopher,' I said. I wondered whether, even now, I could bring a measure of light into his dark mind. 'Yes, you deny an instinctive, imaginative focus through which something is re-built that can never be re-built exactly. In all re-building of what is lost we are in league with a truth beyond ourselves. Thus we gain, or lose, an inch to an *inner* structure that we seek. What is the *creative* imagination? Do we truly know what it is? The inch that we gain, or lose, may tell us much about ourselves, our brokenness, our imperfections, our hopes of perfection, much more than we realise. There is a multiplication of disguises of ourselves in everything we build and re-build.'

I wondered whether I had gained a fraction of an inch in convincing Christopher to turn away from whatever it was he contemplated in his mind. He said nothing. He was evidently deeply puzzled, deeply disturbed.

'Columbus has vanished,' I continued, 'but you seek to bring him back as a guiding pole in your measurements of the past and the present. He is a ghost-figure that wakes in your unconscious. You do not *will* him to be. He arises. That is all you can say. Do you know him? You do in an imperfect realisation of many others that you meet in the journey of life.'

Christopher burst out – to my astonishment – with an adamant remark: 'I tell you it is *my* ship. I have re-built it completely. I shall sail around the Caribbean in it.' He touched his pocket as he spoke as though he were testing a compass within his garment that would make his words come drastically true.

'Have you re-built it?' I said a trifle mockingly. I could not help myself. 'So have the people from the boxing stadium who passed in the street. Columbus came to the Caribbean in 1492 and he was wounded.'

'He was *not*,' Christopher exclaimed.

'He was *blind*,' I insisted, 'a blindness unlike the inner seeing sight of Tiresias! His kind of blindness is a terrible wound. He saw the world in a confusion of continents. He had *technically* circumnavigated a globe in which he had arrived in India whereas he was on islands at the edge of the Americas. This was the supreme imperial blunder. And it was to lead to catastrophe around the world.'

'He saw his way clearly,' Christopher cried.

'Saw his way clearly in the old style of conquest,' I said. I hesitated, not wishing to annoy Christopher unduly. 'I would have thought it necessary', I said softly, 'for him to sense new cross-culturalities in himself – associated with others, with strangers – as he learnt he had arrived *blindly* at the edge of another world of which he knew nothing.' I stopped. I had said enough, I felt.

'I tell you he knew what he was doing,' Christopher said. 'Conquest was inevitable if he were to bring the religion of Christ to a barbarous people.'

94

I hesitated. What could I say which would not cause an outrage, however true it was?

'The barbarism in the arts of the pre-Columbian civilisation', I conceded, 'was intended to release a working, day-to-day dialogue between the conscious and the unconscious, between what rises up in ourselves from the depths and meets the rational surfaces of behaviour that may prove to be nothing but a mask we present to others. Weather-gods, rain-gods, fire-gods, and so on, rise up and speak to the people in their sculptures and paintings. Sometimes evil would appear to have the upper hand, sometimes good. But it was felt deeply – in all shades of perception from dark to light – that evil and good are mysteriously related, that innocence and guilt are also mysteriously related . . .'

Christopher interrupted: 'I do not agree', he said, 'that such relationships exist. One is innocent or guilty. One may wear a mask but that cannot conceal entirely one's innocence or guilt.'

'Yes, I know that is how it seems in Columbian and Western societies, where a rigid pendulum swings between evil and good that are seen as wholly separate. One century the pendulum swings against a particular people (who are deemed to be separate from all others and to be guilty). The next, perhaps it swings in favour of that very people (who are now deemed to be innocent). The swing does not happen within the psyche of the people. It is a purely historical, technical switch. I find it not easy to explain the processes in an utterly different civilisation. I wish I could.'

'What do you mean? Could you give me an example in Western societies?'

I felt he knew of examples but asked the question to try me or to indict me. I trembled within myself and hesitated again. Then I said: 'Take the Jews. Surely everyone knows of their case in Europe. They were blamed and persecuted across hundreds of years for the crucifixion of Christ. No one else confessed to instinctive guilt for the barbarous deed that had been performed by the Roman military.' I hesitated again. Then I said slowly, hesitantly: 'If they had – in a sufficiency of numbers – the Holocaust might never have happened.'

'What do you mean?' Christopher demanded.

'I mean the shocking murder of the Jews in the twentieth century may not have happened.' I continued more rapidly now. I had touched on a subject Christopher would not like. 'If there had been a day-to-day awareness of evil and good as related, and people had seen in themselves what was happening, across the centuries, there could have been a slow dissolution of a mountain of evil which exploded suddenly within one of the most gifted of European peoples who prided themselves on absolute superiority in race and culture. William Blake seems to be a notable exception in Europe . . .'

Christopher interrupted rudely: 'What has William Blake to do with all this? Are you mad? Blake is honoured for his perception of the divine.'

I had gone too far to pull back from my inmost feelings. 'Blake', I said, 'asserted that satanic forces energised eternity and helped the divine into eternity. That is how I read some of the words in his elaborate poems. I confess I may be wrong. He seems a great genius, and perhaps solitary and exceptional. I have nothing more to say about this. I am sorry I have angered you. I have given my opinions. I may be wrong.' This was the best I could do to retrieve the ground I had lost. Christopher looked at me with disdain.

There was a curious sensation of wrath on his face. I had said things I never intended saying. They had arisen in me despite my strict intentions. What could I do now? I knew we were in a play of the conscious and the unconscious through which sculptures spark their anger to make us aware of their enigmatic presence. Could Christopher's wrath be an aspect of the anger of a sculpture which he knew, as he looked into the room the Wanderer had opened, but pretended not to understand? Had anger arisen from the depths of himself? Was he angry with himself?

'There is a ship,' I said, 'which Elena/Medea sees in the dark room the Wanderer brings into the play. We can see what she sees. Do not be angry. It will spoil your appreciation of the myth in which you are involved. The ship is in Herman Melville's *Benito Cereno*. It is a ghost-ship though Melville may not have intended it to be so. Let us look at it with Elena/Medea's eyes appearing in the lines Melville has written:

'The ship, when made signally visible on the verge of the leaden-hued swells, with the shreds of fog here and there raggedly furring her, appeared like a whitewashed monastery after a thunder-storm, seen perched upon some dun cliff among the Pyrenees. But it was no purely fanciful resemblance which now, for a moment, almost led [one] to think that nothing less than a shipload of monks was before [one]. Peering over the bulwarks were what really seemed, in the hazy distance, throngs of dark cowls; while, fitfully, revealed through the open port-holes, other dark moving figures were dimly descried, as of Black Friars pacing the cloisters.

Upon a still nigher approach, the appearance was modified, and the true character of the vessel was plain – a Spanish merchantman of the first class, carrying negro slaves, amongst other valuable freight, from one colonial port to another.'

'The lights are not good,' said Christopher. 'I can scarcely see the ship or the slaves upon it.'

'The slaves would normally be held below in horrible conditions. They are never allowed above. But it is important to see what Elena/Medea sees: a ghost-ship. As such there are many possibilities that hazily project themselves into the present, the past and the future. One is the possibility that what seems fanciful is both real and unreal. Are the black men at the open port-holes truly themselves, truly within themselves, or are they masked and dressed as Black Friars, as a ruling clique within the Church? If they are dressed as Friars they may have come on deck but are still bound in spirit below. They may have lost their originality in a Church or a State which has them mimic, or imprison themselves in, its own cliques but tells them it is liberal, they are free. What is freedom? One is left to calculate how the slaves or mimics of a system everyone is told to admire because it is the best in the world, can find freedom when the system itself enslaves itself by freight, by a lust for money, which banishes originality. A mutiny has occurred on board the ship.

'But the ghost of possibilities within a slave of the system – a slave riding high but imprisoned in the system – looms again and again. Unreality and reality are intermingled in a conflict that leaves us numb and haunted by memories of war . . . Perhaps those memories will bring a change through and beyond the absolutes which tie us down for ever.'

'This is folly – a dangerous folly,' said Christopher. 'This play is dangerous. I must bring it to an end. It must stop! It must stop! Is the Wanderer a Tiger? I see him in the painting like someone waiting to spring.'

And then – without a further word of warning – he put his hand into a pocket and drew forth not a compass but a knife. He looked at me for a quick moment. The knife was uplifted in his hand as though he intended striking at me. But he turned to the canvas on the walls and began to slice and cut into the painting. He sliced into it from wall to wall until it became a series of rags. The broken figures drooped in pieces, it was an alarming spectacle, they were bundled together, they fell to the ground. I wanted to stop him but my arms were void, they were phantom arms. They possessed an independence but were without material force. If they sprang on anyone they became a cloud, a clear day would grow dark with clouds. He sliced the River into broken pavements, he sliced the Forest into broken Arawaks, he sliced the Rooms into lost Cities.

I screamed. I had been broken into bits myself on a wall. I had tried to scream before but nothing had come from my painted throat. At last, however, a mysterious scream rang out loud and clear. It seemed to shake the building. Was the City collapsing within the heart of the painting? It righted itself as though a quake in the soil had passed and left it desolate immediately after the scream.

George and Andy rushed into the room. They held Christopher, who turned on them and said: 'Ask him why I did this! He was talking dangerous folly. The play must stop. *The play must stop!*'

'Ask whom?' they cried.

'Ask him!' He turned to where I had been but there was no one there. I had vanished from the floor of the room. I felt I had sensed a disaster hanging over Christopher's mind but an attack on a work of Art had come as a terrible surprise and I had been bowled over in the rapids of history.

'There is no one here,' said Andy.

He turned to meet three men who had heard the piercing scream and had come from their offices in the building. The police arrived not long after. They seized Christopher and put chains on his wrists.

'I tell you,' Christopher cried, 'I cut the painting to shreds because of the dangerous folly I heard from *him*. I am a peace-loving Christian and I have done my duty. Others may do nothing but they know deeply how I feel.'

'There is no one here,' said an officer. 'He imagines he saw someone. He is insane.'

'Who screamed?' said Andy. 'George and I and everyone in the building heard the scream.'

George and Andy remained in the room bitten, as it were, by profound sadness. They could not believe Christopher had gone for good. Would he not come tomorrow? Would the painting not be here? Andy departed but George remained. He stared at the pieces on the floor. An effort would be made, he knew, to put the painting together once more. There were scraps still on the wall. A green scrap. Tiresias's coat had escaped the knife. It still hung in the broken painting but had been wrinkled into an eye peering at George.

George opened the window and stepped out onto a balcony. It was evening. He remembered Andy saying Christopher had concealed something from him when he spoke of his meeting with Jason, the boxer.

The lights of a constellation were emerging far away in the sky and George wondered whether this bore on what Christopher had concealed. Perhaps he had seen a constellation of the Wanderer waiting to leap.

The constellation that George now saw was burning slightly, it seemed, at its edges and there were marks as well on its distant, bone-like, fiery face. George was stricken with astonishment. Could this be the Wanderer?

It was a skeleton of lights. It may have been there a million and more years before Man had appeared on planet Earth. How could it be anything one now knew? One could clothe it with the garments of myth and legend but these were illusions, they were ruins in which one placed the origins of Art.

George was suddenly empowered by the distant spectrum in the sky. He had wandered the Earth for many years. He was a minimal wanderer who could become a major Wanderer following a skeleton of hazy lights he could not identify.

Was this the immense journey of life? Was it a skeleton to follow through and beyond himself? Was it a Nobody? Was it a Darkness? Whatever it was, it would help him to bring the tattered and bereft figures lying on the floor back into a painting.

He had been empowered to do so by the celestial unconscious. It is real and unreal, and it inspires us to make of illusion a shape which represents an eternity of riddles, a shape brooding upon ruin and unknown fulfilment and origin.